MORA

M000197659

THE BELGRAVE MANOR CRIME

KATHERINE DALTON RENOIR ('Moray Dalton') was born in Hammersmith, London in 1881, the only child of a Canadian father and English mother.

The author wrote two well-received early novels, *Olive in Italy* (1909), and *The Sword of Love* (1920). However, her career in crime fiction did not begin until 1924, after which Moray Dalton published twenty-nine mysteries, the last in 1951. The majority of these feature her recurring sleuths, Scotland Yard inspector Hugh Collier and private inquiry agent Hermann Glide.

Moray Dalton married Louis Jean Renoir in 1921, and the couple had a son a year later. The author lived on the south coast of England for the majority of her life following the marriage. She died in Worthing, West Sussex, in 1963.

MORAY DALTON MYSTERIES
Available from Dean Street Press

MORAY DALTON

THE BELGRAVE MANOR CRIME

With an introduction by Curtis Evans

DEAN STREET PRESS

LOST GOLD FROM A GOLDEN AGE

The Detective Fiction of Moray Dalton
(Katherine Mary Deville Dalton Renoir, 1881-1963)

"GOLD" COMES in many forms. For literal-minded people gold may be merely a precious metal, physically stripped from the earth. For fans of Golden Age detective fiction, however, gold can be artfully spun out of the human brain, in the form not of bricks but books. While the father of Katherine Mary Deville Dalton Renoir may have derived the Dalton family fortune from nuggets of metallic ore, the riches which she herself produced were made from far humbler, though arguably ultimately mightier, materials: paper and ink. As the mystery writer Moray Dalton, Katherine Dalton Renoir published twenty-nine crime novels between 1924 and 1951, the majority of which feature her recurring sleuths, Scotland Yard inspector Hugh Collier and private inquiry agent Hermann Glide. Although the Moray Dalton mysteries are finely polished examples of criminally scintillating Golden Age art, the books unjustifiably fell into neglect for decades. For most fans of vintage mystery they long remained, like the fabled Lost Dutchman's mine, tantalizingly elusive treasure. Happily the crime fiction of Moray Dalton has been unearthed for modern readers by those industrious miners of vintage mystery at Dean Street Press.

Born in Hammersmith, London on May 6, 1881, Katherine was the only child of Joseph Dixon Dalton and Laura Back Dalton. Like the parents of that admittedly more famous mistress of mystery, Agatha Christie, Katherine's parents hailed from different nations, separated by the Atlantic Ocean. While both authors had British mothers, Christie's father was American and Dalton's father Canadian.

Laura Back Dalton, who at the time of her marriage in 1879 was twenty-six years old, about fifteen years younger than her husband, was the daughter of Alfred and Catherine Mary Back. In her early childhood years Laura Back resided at Valley

House, a lovely regency villa built around 1825 in Stratford St. Mary, Suffolk, in the heart of so-called "Constable Country" (so named for the fact that the great Suffolk landscape artist John Constable painted many of his works in and around Stratford). Alfred Back was a wealthy miller who with his brother Octavius, a corn merchant, owned and operated a steam-powered six-story mill right across the River Stour from Valley House. In 1820 John Constable, himself the son of a miller, executed a painting of fishers on the River Stour which partly included the earlier, more modest incarnation (complete with water wheel) of the Back family's mill. (This piece Constable later repainted under the title *The Young Waltonians*, one of his best known works.) After Alfred Back's death in 1860, his widow moved with her daughters to Brondesbury Villas in Maida Vale, London, where Laura in the 1870s met Joseph Dixon Dalton, an eligible Canadian-born bachelor and retired gold miner of about forty years of age who lived in nearby Kew.

Joseph Dixon Dalton was born around 1838 in London, Ontario, Canada, to Henry and Mary (Dixon) Dalton, Wesleyan Methodists from northern England who had migrated to Canada a few years previously. In 1834, not long before Joseph's birth, Henry Dalton started a soap and candle factory in London, Ontario, which after his death two decades later was continued, under the appellation Dalton Brothers, by Joseph and his siblings Joshua and Thomas. (No relation to the notorious "Dalton Gang" of American outlaws is presumed.) Joseph's sister Hannah wed John Carling, a politician who came from a prominent family of Canadian brewers and was later knighted for his varied public services, making him Sir John and his wife Lady Hannah. Just how Joseph left the family soap and candle business to prospect for gold is currently unclear, but sometime in the 1870s, after fabulous gold rushes at Cariboo and Cassiar, British Columbia and the Black Hills of South Dakota, among other locales, Joseph left Canada and carried his riches with him to London, England, where for a time he enjoyed life as a gentleman of leisure in one of the great metropolises of the world.

Although Joshua and Laura Dalton's first married years were spent with their daughter Katherine in Hammersmith at a villa named Kenmore Lodge, by 1891 the family had moved to 9 Orchard Place in Southampton, where young Katherine received a private education from Jeanne Delport, a governess from Paris. Two decades later, Katherine, now 30 years old, resided with her parents at Perth Villa in the village of Merriott, Somerset, today about an eighty miles' drive west of Southampton. By this time Katherine had published, under the masculine-sounding pseudonym of Moray Dalton (probably a gender-bending play on "Mary Dalton") a well-received first novel, *Olive in Italy* (1909), a study of a winsome orphaned Englishwoman attempting to make her own living as an artist's model in Italy that possibly had been influenced by E.M. Forster's novels *Where Angels Fear to Tread* (1905) and *A Room with a View* (1908), both of which are partly set in an idealized Italy of pure gold sunlight and passionate love. Yet despite her accomplishment, Katherine's name had no occupation listed next it in the census two years later.

During the Great War the Daltons, parents and child, resided at 14 East Ham Road in Littlehampton, a seaside resort town located 19 miles west of Brighton. Like many other bookish and patriotic British women of her day, Katherine produced an effusion of memorial war poetry, including "To Some Who Have Fallen," "Edith Cavell," "Rupert Brooke," "To Italy" and "Mort Homme." These short works appeared in the *Spectator* and were reprinted during and after the war in George Herbert Clarke's *Treasury of War Poetry* anthologies. "To Italy," which Katherine had composed as a tribute to the beleaguered British ally after its calamitous defeat, at the hands of the forces of Germany and Austria-Hungary, at the Battle of Caporetto in 1917, even popped up in the United States in the "poet's corner" of the *United Mine Workers Journal*, perhaps on account of the poem's pro-Italy sentiment, doubtlessly agreeable to Italian miner immigrants in America.

Katherine also published short stories in various periodicals, including *The Cornhill Magazine*, which was then edited by Leonard Huxley, son of the eminent zoologist Thomas Henry Huxley and father of famed writer Aldous Huxley. Leonard Huxley obligingly read over--and in his words "plied my scalpel upon"--Katherine's second novel, *The Sword of Love*, a romantic adventure saga set in the Florentine Republic at the time of Lorenzo the Magnificent and the infamous Pazzi Conspiracy, which was published in 1920. Katherine writes with obvious affection for *il bel paese* in her first two novels and her poem "To Italy," which concludes with the ringing lines

> Greece was enslaved, and Carthage is but dust,
> But thou art living, maugre [i.e., in spite of] all thy scars,
> To bear fresh wounds of rapine and of lust,
> Immortal victim of unnumbered wars.
> Nor shalt thou cease until we cease to be
> Whose hearts are thine, beloved Italy.

The author maintained her affection for "beloved Italy" in her later Moray Dalton mysteries, which include sympathetically-rendered Italian settings and characters.

Around this time Katherine in her own life evidently discovered romance, however short-lived. At Brighton in the spring of 1921, the author, now nearly 40 years old, wed a presumed Frenchman, Louis Jean Renoir, by whom the next year she bore her only child, a son, Louis Anthony Laurence Dalton Renoir. (Katherine's father seems to have missed these important developments in his daughter's life, apparently having died in 1918, possibly in the flu pandemic.) Sparse evidence as to the actual existence of this man, Louis Jean Renoir, in Katherine's life suggests that the marriage may not have been a successful one. In the 1939 census Katherine was listed as living with her mother Laura at 71 Wallace Avenue in Worthing, Sussex, another coastal town not far from Brighton, where she had married Louis Jean eighteen years earlier; yet he is not in evidence, even though he is stated to be Katherine's husband in her mother's will, which was probated in Worthing in 1945. Perhaps not unrelatedly, empathy with what people in her day considered unorthodox sexual unions characterizes the crime fiction which Katherine would write.

Whatever happened to Louis Jean Renoir, marriage and motherhood did not slow down "Moray Dalton." Indeed, much to the contrary, in 1924, only a couple of years after the birth of her son, Katherine published, at the age of 42 (the same age at which P.D. James published her debut mystery novel, *Cover Her Face*), *The Kingsclere Mystery*, the first of her 29 crime novels. (Possibly the title was derived from the village of Kingsclere, located some 30 miles north of Southampton.) The heady scent of Renaissance romance which perfumes *The Sword of Love* is found as well in the first four Moray Dalton mysteries (aside from *The Kingsclere Mystery*, these are *The Shadow on the Wall*, *The Black Wings* and *The Stretton Darknesse Mystery*), which although set in the present-day world have, like much of the mystery fiction of John Dickson Carr, the elevated emotional temperature of the highly-colored age of the cavaliers. However in 1929 and 1930, with the publication of, respectively, *One by One They Disappeared*, the first of the Inspector Hugh Collier mysteries and *The Body in the Road*, the debut Hermann Glide tale, the Moray Dalton novels begin to become more typical of British crime fiction at that time, ultimately bearing considerable similarity to the work of Agatha Christie and Dorothy L. Sayers, as well as other prolific women mystery authors who would achieve popularity in the 1930s, such as Margery Allingham, Lucy Beatrice Malleson (best known as "Anthony Gilbert") and Edith Caroline Rivett, who wrote under the pen names E.C.R. Lorac and Carol Carnac.

For much of the decade of the 1930s Katherine shared the same publisher, Sampson Low, with Edith Rivett, who published her first detective novel in 1931, although Rivett moved on, with both of her pseudonyms, to that rather more prominent purveyor of mysteries, the Collins Crime Club. Consequently the Lorac and Carnac novels are better known today than those of Moray Dalton. Additionally, only three early Moray Dalton titles (*One by One They Disappeared*, *The Body in the Road* and *The Night of Fear*) were picked up in the United States, another factor which mitigated against the Dalton mysteries achieving long-term renown. It is also possible that the independently wealthy author, who left an estate valued, in modern estimation, at nearly a million American dollars at her death at the age of 81 in 1963, felt less of an imperative to "push" her writing than the typical "starving author."

Whatever forces compelled Katherine Dalton Renoir to write fiction, between 1929 and 1951 the author as Moray Dalton published fifteen Inspector Hugh Collier mysteries and ten other crime novels (several of these with Hermann Glide). Some of the non-series novels daringly straddle genres. *The Black Death*, for example, somewhat bizarrely yet altogether compellingly merges the murder mystery with post-apocalyptic science fiction, whereas *Death at the Villa*, set in Italy during the Second World War, is a gripping wartime adventure thriller with crime and death. Taken together, the imaginative and ingenious Moray Dalton crime fiction, wherein death is not so much a game as a dark and compelling human drama, is one of the more significant bodies of work by a Golden Age mystery writer—though the author has, until now, been most regrettably overlooked by publishers, for decades remaining accessible almost solely to connoisseurs with deep pockets.

Even noted mystery genre authorities Jacques Barzun and Wendell Hertig Taylor managed to read only five books by Moray Dalton, all of which the pair thereupon listed in their massive critical compendium, *A Catalogue of Crime* (1972; revised and expanded 1989). Yet Barzun and Taylor were warm admirers of the author's writing, avowing for example, of the twelfth Hugh Collier mystery, *The Condamine Case* (under the impression that the author was a man): "[T]his is the author's 17th book, and [it is] remarkably fresh and unstereotyped [actually it was Dalton's 25th book, making it even more remarkable—C.E.]. . . . [H]ere is a neglected man, for his earlier work shows him to be a conscientious workman, with a flair for the unusual, and capable of clever touches."

Today in 2019, nine decades since the debut of the conscientious and clever Moray Dalton's Inspector Hugh Collier detective series, it is a great personal pleasure to announce that this criminally neglected woman is neglected no longer and to welcome her books back into light. Vintage crime fiction fans have a golden treat in store with the classic mysteries of Moray Dalton.

The Belgrave Manor Crime

MY COPY of Moray Dalton's *The Belgrave Manor Crime*--it is the fifth Inspector Hugh Collier novel, first published in 1935, and a companion volume of sorts to *The Belfry Murder* (1933) --has a stamp from Blackdown High School, located on Park Road in Leamington Spa, a lovely small city in Warwickshire. This locale is not, I imagine, all that dissimilar from the author's favored settings in southern England. Belgrave Manor, the sinister locus of the novel, is located near Lewes in East Sussex, the area where Dalton spent most of her life.

The Belgrave Manor Crime opens with a new character in the Moray Dalton crime novel corpus (at least I had not encountered him before): psychic investigator Cosmo Thor. (You know he has to be a psychic investigator with a name like Cosmo Thor.) He was not actually a stranger to faithful Dalton readers, however. Cosmo Thor originally appeared in a series of six short stories published between July and December 1927 in *Premier Magazine*, under the title "The Strange Cases of Cosmo Thor," wherein Thor features as "a detective with remarkable empathy and insight," according to *The Encyclopedia of Science Fiction*. As such Cosmo Thor followed in the tradition of such fictional psychic, or occult, sleuths as John Bell, Flaxman Low, Algernon Blackwood's John Silence, William Hope Hodgson's Carnacki and F. Tennyson Jesse's Solange Fontaine, the first woman to join this investigative company.

In *The Belgrave Manor Crime* Moray Dalton describes Thor as "an authority on what had hitherto been a kind of No Man's Land between that covered by the C.I.D. and the alienist." When the story opens, the psychic investigator, returning to London by train from a case in the Midlands, encounters a young palmist he knows, a certain Madame Luna, who has been released from jail after three weeks for over zealously practicing her mystical art. A police "trap," she explains, led her into predicting more about the future than she should have.

The palmist informs Thor that she is on her way to get back to her little girl, Allie, whom she left in the care of her landlady while she was incarcerated. After parting ways with Madame Luna and arriving in London, Thor resolves to take a restful weekend in the country. On returning home, he learns from his not overly bright landlady (much in the tradition of landladies in Golden Age crime fiction) that a visibly distressed Madame Luna had desperately wanted to see him over the weekend, but was turned away. Concerned, Thor consults his policeman friend, Hugh Collier, and learns from him that Madame Luna may be the woman who was found dead from a fall from a cliff in Devon. But what in this world (or the next) was Madame Luna doing on a cliff in Devon, if the dead woman indeed was she?

Thor's investigation ultimately leads him to Belgrave Manor, a Sussex country house of ill-favored reputation to the inhabitants of the nearby village of Mitre Gap. After a long abandonment, Thor learns from local father-and-son house agents John and Dennis Garland, Belgrave Manor was purchased by wealthy London philanthropist Mrs. Maulfrey. It was to Belgrave Manor which Mrs. Maulfrey, who unexpectedly asserted custody over Madame Luna's daughter Allie while her mother was incarcerated, sent her young charge, in care of a pretty young governess, Miss Celia Kent (does that name remind you of anyone?), with whom Dennis has become rather smitten.

After a tense visit to Belgrave Manor, Cosmo Thor is sidelined from the case, but fortunately intrepid Hugh Collier is on hand to pick up the threads in what turns out to be a remarkably sinister case, one in which Hugh himself will be put in grave peril of his life. If you do not like Hugh Collier by now, you certainly should after reading this story. He is a good bloke indeed, most determined to do justice unto the innocent and the guilty, whatever their station, even to the point of butting heads, if necessary, with his more hesitant superiors, Chief-Inspector Cardew and Assistant Commissioner Sir James Mercer, as he had previously done in *The Belfry Murder*.

Admittedly, *The Belgrave Manor Crime* is more of a thriller than a detective novel, although there is detection (as well as a rather nasty series of murders). Yet it is a terrifically enjoyable one, richer than most of the plethora of Edgar Wallace and sub-Wallace "shockers" that were published in this period. I am reminded of the Thirties mysteries which Margery Allingham wrote under her pseudonym "Maxwell March." The story actually gets rather dark (especially for the period), and, as with other Daltons, it is easy for me to imagine its being filmed by modern movie makers who like "darkness" in their mysteries. *Belgrave* is an impressive tale of outré mystery and lurid crime, with a cast of compelling characters, both good and bad.

And, be warned my dear readers: when those bad characters are bad, they are horrid!

Curtis Evans

Chapter I
MADAME LUNA

"OH, MR. Thor—don't you remember me?"

Thor, who had spent the last hour in the restaurant car, had resumed his seat with only a casual glance at the woman who had established herself in the seat facing his during his absence. Now that she had spoken he recognised her. He had been spending a few days at an East coast resort at the close of the summer season two years previously. She had been doing palmistry at the end of the pier, but clients had been few and she was in pitiful straits. Thor, seeing her wan little face peering wistfully out of her booth, had given her five shillings, double her usual fee, for a hand reading; and, after hearing her story, had paid her debts and helped her to get back to London.

He had neither seen her nor heard from her since. He was a serious student of the occult, and, as such, he sometimes regretted the traffic in amulets and horoscopes carried on by the possessors of a small psychic gift who picked up a precarious living on the fringes of the spiritualist movement; but he knew their difficulties and their temptations, and he would always help them if he could. He was a man of independent means, and, since his mother's death, with no family ties. He had spent some years in the East. On his return he had taken a flat in a block off Vincent Square, where he lived with an old family servant as his housekeeper. He was gradually becoming known as an authority on what had hitherto been a kind of No Man's Land between that covered by the C.I.D. and the alienist. Though he prided himself on never turning away a client in real need of his help he only undertook cases that made an appeal either to his scientific curiosity, or to a heart that was softer than his lean, harsh-featured face and his aloof manner indicated. He had just concluded an enquiry in the Midlands and he was conscious of both bodily and mental fatigue, but there was nothing in his manner to betray the fact that he would rather have been left to doze in his corner until the outskirts of London were reached.

"Of course I remember you," he said, smiling.

She had not altered much. A little shabbier perhaps and more shrunken. Living on her nerves, he thought, and on not much else.

"I hope you are doing better now," he said.

"I was," she said. "I've been developing as a medium, and I made some good friends. But I was engaged to do palmistry at a bazaar up in Manchester. My landlady there persuaded me to stay on a week. She said lots of her friends would come to me. Well, several did—and then—I shall never know who complained to the police, but someone did. They sent a policeman's wife and sister to ask a lot of questions, and I was led into saying more than I should. A trap. Well," she added, with a bitter little laugh, "I suppose I may think myself lucky. I might have had three months, and they only gave me three weeks in the first division. I told them I had my little girl depending on me, I wouldn't have minded so much if it hadn't been for her."

"There was someone to look after her in your absence?"

"My landlady. She's not a bad sort, but easy going."

"You are going back to her now?"

Madame Luna's worn little face lit up, and for an instant she looked quite pretty. "She's everything to me," she said.

"How old is she?"

"Five."

"A pretty age," said Thor. "You must let me help you again. I seem to have brought you luck last time since you found friends after our meeting. Perhaps I shall bring you luck again." He took out his pocket book and extracted ten one pound notes.

"Don't worry about repayment. Let me hear from you if there is anything I can do."

The tired brown eyes of the little palmist filled with tears.

"You're too kind," she faltered.

The train was entering Euston. There was no time for more. She tried to kiss his hand but he prevented her. The last he saw of her she was toiling down the platform, weighed down by her suit-case. A porter was collecting his luggage and his attention was distracted. When he glanced round again she had disappeared in the crowd.

He secured a taxi and drove back to his flat. Mrs. Jeal received him with head shakings. She had never overcome her disapproval of his activities. "You look worn out, Mr. Cosmo. I wish folk'd leave you alone. You want a rest."

He was glancing through the letters that had come for him by the morning post. "I'll take a long week-end off anyhow," he said. "The Willetts have asked me down to Sharings."

The old woman beamed. "Ah, there won't be no trouble there."

The Willetts were a placid, prosperous couple, devoted to their three charming children—Thor was godfather to the youngest—and to their garden. Thor came back to London on Tuesday, having spent most of his waking hours under a cedar on the lawn.

He was feeling decidedly better.

"Any callers?"

Mrs. Jeal answered reluctantly. "There was one. A person calling herself Madame Loony, or some such name."

She had brought her master's tea into the sitting-room and was standing by while he poured out his first cup.

Thor looked up at her quickly. "Madame Luna? What did she want?"

He was frowning slightly. He had given the woman ten pounds. He had not expected her to appeal to him again so soon.

"She didn't say. She came not an hour after you left on Friday, asking to see you. Very flustered, she seemed, and as white as a sheet. I told her it was no use, that you'd gone on holiday."

"What did she say to that?"

Mrs. Jeal showed a trace of embarrassment. "She seemed upset."

Thor's manner hardened. "I want a plain answer. What did she say?"

The old housekeeper answered sulkily. "She said 'My God! Can't I get at him?' and I said, 'You can call again Tuesday evening. He'll be here then,' I said, 'but for the present he's taking a rest. He's flesh and blood like other folk,' I said, but I doubt if she heard me. She was off down the stairs."

"You should, have asked her to wait while you rang me up at Sharings," said her master sternly.

"I'm sorry," she muttered, "but I wanted you to have a rest from them all. They're always after you with this and that."

"I know you meant well," he said more gently, "but you must not try to stand between me and my work. Well—she may call this evening. Show her in if she does."

But Madame Luna did not come again.

Thor was troubled by her non-appearance. He had done his best for her, he had no responsibility, and yet he felt responsible. He had told her to come to him. He was thinking of her when the bell rang the following evening. It was rather late. He had just left his tiny dining-room, and Mrs. Jeal was preparing the coffee. He heard her go to the door, but the visitor she ushered in was a man, Inspector Hugh Collier, of the Criminal Investigation Department at Scotland Yard.

Some time previously a case of alleged haunting which Thor had been asked to investigate had proved to be a fraud intended to mask a cunningly contrived murder. Thor had communicated with the Yard. During the trial at which he had appeared as a witness for the Crown he had met the young Inspector. The two had become excellent friends, and though weeks often passed without their meeting Collier was sure to find his way sooner or later to Vincent Square.

"You were expecting somebody? I'm not butting in?" said Collier as they shook hands.

"Not at all. But how did you know?"

"Your housekeeper told me. Her face fell so perceptibly when she opened the door and saw that it was only an arm of the law," said Collier, smiling. "I don't think she cares much for policemen, even in mufti."

He broke off as Mrs. Jeal came in with the coffee. Her manner was unusually subdued. "You'll see the—Madam Luna—if she comes, sir?"

"Of course."

When she had left them Thor turned to the younger man. "I'd rather like to tell you about this—unofficially," he said.

"Is it in—in your special line?" asked Collier. "You know I've never touched any of this occult stuff, though I've got an open mind and all that."

"No, no. It's, as far as I know, a material dilemma." Thor went on to describe his first meeting with the palmist on the pier at Salthaven and the second in the train a few days previously, and her subsequent call at the flat.

Collier listened attentively, lying back in one of his host's comfortable chairs, sipping his excellent coffee, and smoking a much better cigar than he could himself afford. He had had a hard day at the Yard and he was glad to relax, but if his friend wanted his help he was ready to give it.

He reflected a minute before he made any comment.

"I gather she's an hysterical neurotic type. Perhaps being tearful and exclamatory doesn't mean much in her case," he suggested. "For instance, she might have found there were still some bills owing when she'd spent your ten pounds, and thought she'd touch you for another fiver. Since you were away she may have found another friend to tide her over. Probably that's all there is to it."

"You may be right," said Thor. "I hope you are. But did I say she was hysterical and neurotic? I don't think she is. Impulsive, certainly, and with the lack of poise that comes from living from hand to mouth. And three weeks of square meals in prison hadn't made up for years of under-nourishment. She's a pathetic little soul, Collier, and as honest as she can afford to be I am certain."

The man from the Yard shook his head. "If you knew as much about the seamy side as I do, sir."

"I do know a little," Thor said grimly.

"Well—what do you want me to do?"

Thor hesitated. "I hardly know. If I had her address I'd go and see her. I've looked in the advertising columns of *Light* and all the other papers, but she's not in any of them. I suppose after a conviction for fortune telling she would have to lie low for a while."

"She certainly would. What are you afraid of? That she'll turn on the gas—something of that sort?"

Thor nodded. "She's got her child to support, and she's devoted to her. I'm worried about her, Collier."

"I'll find her for you," said the young detective. "Could you give me a short description?"

Thor complied and Collier scribbled some notes in his book.

"Sounds like nine women out of ten," he said pessimistically. "This standardised ready-made clothing is the devil. Well, I'll do my best to round her up for you, but I hope she comes back of her own accord to set your mind at rest."

He called again three evenings later.

"Any news?"

"No," said Thor.

"I see," Collier hesitated a moment. "There's a woman's body been found at the foot of a cliff in south Devon. I'm afraid—she sounds uncommonly like your Madame Luna. She hasn't been identified. Here's the account in the local paper. I'll read it, shall I?"

"Please," said Thor.

"ANOTHER FATALITY ON BARME HEAD

"The absence of a warning notice and an adequate railing along the cliff edge is believed to have caused the death of the woman whose body was found last Sunday afternoon on the rocks three hundred feet below. There was a train excursion to Barme on Saturday and the deceased is supposed to have come with it. Her handbag is believed to have been washed out to sea as her body would have been if it had not become wedged in a cleft of rock. There were no marks on her underclothing. She is described as between thirty and forty, about five feet three inches in height, ill-nourished, short black hair, unwaved, brown eyes, three teeth missing in lower jaw. No scars but mark of a recent burn on the forefinger of her right hand."

"I don't know about the burn, but the rest of the description tallies with yours."

"I remember now," said Thor, "she burnt her finger while we were talking. She was lighting a cigarette and she did not blow out the match quick enough. She was very on edge then, hardly knew what she was doing. It was on Friday afternoon she came here, very agitated. Suicide? What was she doing at Barme?"

"This woman may not be Madame Luna," said Collier. "I wish I'd known before. The inquest is over now and she's been buried."

"What was the coroner's verdict?"

"Oh, accidental, and a rider from the jury about putting up a fence. Of course it may be O.K. There was a good deal of mist along the coast at the time."

"Well, I'll have a look round," said Thor.

"You will?" Collier's tone betrayed his satisfaction. "I'm glad. Between you and me that sort of accident isn't very good for a place and is too apt to be glossed over. We can't butt in unasked, you know, but you, being a free lance—even so you'll have to handle the local police carefully."

Thor smiled faintly. "I probably shan't go near them. But in most of my cases I have to steer a difficult course between the Scylla of medical etiquette and the Charybdis of the law. And I don't really think this poor woman can be Madame Luna."

CHAPTER II
THE RESULT OF AN ACCIDENT

THOR reached Barme soon after noon and had lunch at the Dolphin down by the quay. It was not difficult to induce the landlord to discuss the recent tragedy. He had been foreman of the jury at the inquest. Thor soon saw that it had never occurred to him that the woman's death might not be accidental. A boy had fallen over at the same spot two years previously, trying to reach a bird's nest. His body had been carried away by the tide and washed up in a cove on the western side of Barme Head.

"The fishermen say anything that falls off the Head's bound to fetch up there. 'Tis the currents."

"After how long?"

"Two or three days mostly. The farmer loses a sheep that way sometimes. Will you have coffee, sir?"

Thor, with some experience of coffee in English inns, declined. "I want to retain the flavour of your excellent cider," he said with a smile.

The landlord was gratified. "Will you be wanting a room, sir?"

"I'm not sure yet. I may have to return to Town to-night. I'll leave my bag here. I'll climb the Head and be back for tea."

Thor had decided to take Collier's hint and steer clear of the police station for the present at any rate. He was not likely to learn much from the pathetic little heap of sodden and blood-stained clothing that was all they had to show him now.

He left the little fishing village drowsing in the afternoon sunshine and climbed the steep slope of thyme-scented turf to Barme Head.

When he reached the top he saw that other paths converged, winding through patches of gorse and brambles, to where a seat had been placed for visitors to rest and enjoy the view. He sat for a minute admiring the great sweep of sea and sky from Portland Bill to Start Point before he unfolded his ordnance map. Larks were singing overhead. There was no other human being in sight. A few yards on his left a flimsy pitch pine railing and a notice board marked Danger indicated that the local authorities had taken the rider of the coroner's jury to heart.

He studied the map.

The Head could be reached by climbing the footpath from the village, but there was also a road crossing the Head before it turned again in-land which did not touch the village at all, a road that was probably used by motorists picnicking on the cliffs.

Thor got up and began to wander about in an apparently aimless manner, pausing now and again to glance about him and poking in the undergrowth with his stick. In this way he reached the field gate opening on the road. He noticed a blackened patch on the grass by the roadside made by droppings of oil from a standing car. He glanced back. The distance from the edge of the cliff was about a hundred yards by a well trodden path. As he turned he noticed a scrap of cardboard caught in the furze close to the gate. He stooped to pick it up. It was the unused return half of a third class ticket from Victoria to Lewes.

He went back to the seat and sat down again, but not before he had looked over the edge of the cliff into the sandy cove to which the landlord of the Dolphin had referred. The receding tide had left a narrow brown line of seaweed and nothing more. When he returned to the inn he found that a sumptuous tea had been laid for him on a table under an apple tree in the back garden. The landlord himself brought out the teapot and the plate of hot splits.

"A nice view up there, sir."

"Very. But I couldn't help thinking of that poor woman. It's strange that no one has claimed her."

"That's what I said to the sergeant, sir, him and me being friendly. His wife's sister married my aunt's son. But he says there's a terrible lot of women living alone in flats and doing their own work who can disappear and nobody be any the wiser."

"That's true. But if she came down on an excursion there must have been a good many people about. It's a wonder no one saw her fall over."

"Not as it happened, sir. Usually when the railway runs a trip to Sandport Junction most of the folks find their way here before they leave, but that day a thick fog came rolling up from the sea round about noon so that after hanging about a bit waiting for it to clear most of them spent the afternoon at the Sandport Picture House. A few that was hardier or more hopeful got down here. We supplied five or six parties with teas and warned them all to keep to the road going back."

"I see," said Thor, "then you think she lost her way in the fog?"

"That's right." The landlord lowered his voice. "Between you and me, sir, it's a scandal that the path hasn't been railed in before, but the gentleman that owns the land up there owns most of the village, and we can't quarrel with our bread and butter."

"Quite."

Thor paid for his tea and hired the Dolphin's battered Ford to convey him to the station. He did not think there was anything more to be learned at Barme. He spent the night at Exeter and reached home soon after noon the next day.

He found a scribbled pencil scrawl from Collier.

"I'm being sent to Hamburg, and I may have to go on to the States. I've got Madame Luna's last London address for you. 18 Galen Street, Pimlico, but there's a newsagent and sweet shop on the ground floor, and she may have only had letters there. Good hunting. H.C."

Galen Street was within a quarter of an hour's walk of Vincent Square. It proved to be a grey and grimy thoroughfare.

Lean cats skulked in the areas. Some of the windows displaying cards announcing that a bedsitting-room was to let were heavily curtained with tawdry lace. Thor went into the little newsagent's shop at the corner and bought a packet of postcards. He was served by a slatternly girl of fifteen.

"Can I see Madame Luna?"

She eyed him suspiciously. "No, you can't. She's left."

"May I have her present address?"

She raised her voice. "Ma! Here's somebody after Madame what-is-it."

A fat and frowsty woman waddled into the shop. She stared at Thor with wary little eyes deep sunk in fat, and waited for him to speak.

"Madame Luna had rooms in your house?"

"She had a room. What of it?"

"I want to see her."

"It's no manner of use coming here about her," said the fat woman. "I've always tried to keep my house respectable. A lady may have visitors if she behaves as such; that's no affair of mine. I'm not nosey. But leave her kid on my hands and then cut up rough because I let one of her fine friends take charge of her is going a bit too far. Coming back here and saying I didn't ought to have allowed it. The cheek of it. What do you think this house is, I said, a blasted crêche? What's the matter with you? I said. The kid's enjoying country air and what not, and if you want her back you've only got to go to your fine friends and ask for her. And if it comes to that, I said, I know where you've been spending the last three weeks, Madame. Doris saw all about it in the Sunday paper. Only there it said you'd got three months. And what about what you owe me for the kid's keep until she was taken away?"

"One moment," said Thor, "let me get this right. Madame Luna came here last Thursday?"

"That's right. Thursday, wasn't it, Doris?" The girl nodded.

Thor resumed. "She was surprised and annoyed because someone had come during her absence and had taken away her little girl, whom she had left in your charge?"

The fat woman looked him up and down. "See here, mister, what business is it of yours, anyway? If you've been sent to try and put me in the wrong you can blooming well hop it before I calls my Bert to put you out of my shop."

"You misunderstand me," said Thor blandly. "I am quite sure from what you say that you did your best for all concerned. Madame Luna is impulsive. She didn't stop to think. I gather that there was some unpleasantness when she arrived here last Thursday, and that she left and has not been back since."

His calm manner was not without its effect in abating the fat woman's stridency. She answered more quietly:

"That's right. We had words. Mind you, looking back, I can see she might be upset at not finding the kid here. She's a nice kid is little Allie, no life and go like what my children had, but a good little soul in her peaky way. Madame wouldn't let her play in the street. She was shut up in the bedroom all day with her toys. A dull life for a child, if you ask me."

"And a friend of Madame Luna called and took her away?" said Thor. "Did she give any name?"

"Maud Fry, she said. Mrs. Maud Fry. An oldish woman, dressed in black, but good black, mind you. Tall she was, and as thin as a rake. A dark, foreign-looking person, but very pleasant, and a very posh car outside with a shover and all. I said to my daughter afterwards, 'The kid's in luck,' didn't I, Dorrie?"

"Did she leave you her address?"

"Well, no, she didn't. She said she'd heard Madame was in trouble and she was prepared to look after Allie for the time being, I fetched the kid down and she said, 'Never mind about her clothes. I'll buy her some new ones. Isn't she a little darling.'"

A light broke upon Thor. He knew who Madame Luna's friend was. Not Maud Fry, but Maulfry. He had met her once or twice. A wealthy woman, the widow of a man who had made his fortune in—had it been rubber or South American rails? She was known to take an interest in occultism, and had been for a while a member of the Psychical Research Society. She gave largely to charities and was identified with many good causes. Her descent upon Galen Street was quite in character. Thor, who had begun to suspect he knew not what, was relieved.

Whatever the fate of the mother, little Allie was in good hands. But why then had Madame Luna come to him on the Friday, white-faced and shaking with either anger or fear?

He thanked his interlocutrix, and left the shop. As he walked down the dreary street where the children, just out of school, were playing in the gutter, he was inclined to agree that little Allie had been in luck and that any change from Galen Street must be a change for the better. But what was to become of the child if she was now, as he feared, motherless? Would Mrs. Maulfry adopt her altogether?

Obviously his next step must be to call on the lady and see if she could throw any light on the problem. He went back to his flat for a cup of tea and a cigarette and looked up her address in the directory. Half an hour later he was standing on her doorstep. Mrs. Maulfry lived in Swan Walk. Her house, dating back to the reign of Queen Anne, had conserved the air of spacious dignity belonging to that period. Its windows overlooked the old herb garden. An impassive manservant took Thor's card and left him in a small room on the left of the entrance hall while he went to see if his mistress would receive him.

Thor glanced about him with some curiosity. He really knew very little of the woman he had come to see. But the furniture was as lacking in character as that of a doctor's waiting-room. After a moment the door opened and a sandy-haired young woman in a severely tailored navy blue coat and skirt came in hurriedly.

"I beg your pardon. I didn't know there was any one here. I came back for my notes."

She crossed the room to a bureau and was unlocking it as Mrs. Maulfry entered.

"What are you doing, Miss Cole? It is past five."

"I forgot my notes of what you wanted to say at the committee meeting to-morrow. I can type them at home. There won't be time in the morning."

"I see. Don't let it happen again. You know I like you to leave at the proper time."

"Yes, Mrs. Maulfry."

The sandy-haired young woman collected her notes and departed, with a sidelong glance of cool grey-green eyes at Thor. She seemed quite unperturbed by her employer's obvious irritation.

Mrs. Maulfry turned to Thor. "We have met, haven't we, and I know you quite well by reputation," she said graciously, "do sit down." Her voice and manner were cordial but she did not offer her hand. Thor was to learn later that she never shook hands with anyone. Catarina Gomez, in the days of her girlhood in the distant island of Haiti, had been dazzlingly beautiful. The framework of that beauty remained, but the great flashing black eyes were sunken, the white skin stained and withered. It was difficult to guess at her age. She was wearing a dress of black lace with long, transparent sleeves. Diamonds gleamed through the net that veiled her throat, and on her fingers.

"I have come," Thor began, "about Madame Luna. I gathered that she has been one of your protégées—"

There was something, an immobility, about Mrs. Maulfry, that seemed to indicate that this opening was unexpected and possibly unwelcome. After a pause she said, "Did she tell you so? When?"

"I heard it only to-day, but not from her," he said, "and of your great kindness to her little girl."

"I try to help when I can," she murmured. "Life has not used her well."

"She was fortunate at any rate in finding a friend in you," said Thor. "She called on me the other day, but unluckily I was out. My housekeeper told me she was in great distress. Did she come to you?"

"When was this?"

"Friday week."

"Yes. She came here. She was, as you say, distressed. She seemed to think that after her conviction for fortune telling she would be unable to carry on her profession as a palmist. I tried to encourage her. I promised to look after her little girl. I advised her to have a few weeks' rest by the seaside, and I gave her a little money. I thought I might find her some employment. She was very grateful and she promised to write and let me know how she was getting on, but I have not heard from her yet."

Thor's face fell. "Then you don't know where she is now?"

"No. I advised her to go to some quiet place by the sea where she could rest and recuperate. She was evidently on the verge of a nervous breakdown. I did my best to soothe her."

"I am sure you did. Did she threaten to put an end to her life?"

"Yes. But I didn't take that seriously."

"I am afraid she carried out her threat," said Thor.

Mrs. Maulfry uttered an exclamation of horror.

"How? Where?"

"The body of a woman answering to her description was found a few days ago at the foot of a cliff in South Devon. Nobody came forward to identify her and it is believed locally that her death was accidental, but I'm afraid—" He did not finish the sentence.

"But this is terrible!" cried Mrs. Maulfry, "Terrible. Are you quite certain?"

"I am not. I went down, but not until after the funeral. I may be mistaken. I hope I am."

"I hope so too."

Thor reflected.

"Did she see her little girl when she called here on Friday?"

"No. I had engaged a governess to take charge of the child and sent them into the country."

"I see," said Thor. "I wonder why she did not come round on Thursday evening. When I met her in the train she was going straight to her lodgings. Why didn't she come directly to you when she heard from her landlady that the little girl was staying with you? She knew where you lived, I suppose? But, of course, since she came the next morning—"

"Does it matter?" asked Mrs. Maulfry with a touch of impatience.

"She quarrelled with her landlady and did not return there."

"I imagine she went to friends. She did not say. She was very nervy, but I don't think you need worry, Mr. Thor. If she writes to me before she comes back to London I will let you know. You frightened me for the moment with your story of the woman who fell over the cliff, but it cannot be Luna. She would not be so foolish. In any case you need have no anxiety about Allie. I have made myself responsible."

She stood up and bowed, without offering her hand. Thor took the hint. The butler was in the hall, waiting to show him out. It was all quite satisfactory. But—as Thor hesitated, uncertain which way to turn, he felt instinctively that he was being watched, and that the eyes that looked down at him through the fine mesh of Mrs. Maulfry's expensive net curtains were not friendly to him. Involuntarily he shivered. Short as the interview had been he felt tired and chilled as if he had been sitting too long.

As he walked on in the direction of the river he wondered if he should pursue the matter further. The child, at any rate, was provided for. She would have a better start in life than her mother could have given her. Shut up day after day with a few cheap toys in a dingy bed-sitting-room. She was all right. But—

Madame Luna had been in trouble when she came to his flat. And among the torn papers in the basket by the secretary's desk there had been an envelope with the Lewes postmark.

Thor, who had very good eyes, had seen it as he sat waiting for Mrs. Maulfry. It might, of course, be only a coincidence that he had found an unused ticket from Lewes to Victoria on Barme Head within a hundred yards of the spot where the woman whom he believed to have been Madame Luna had fallen to her death, but Thor did not think so.

Chapter III
LET BY GARLAND AND SON

At breakfast the next morning Thor informed his housekeeper that he was going down to Lewes. He might be back that night or he might be away for some days. He would be driving himself down and taking a suit-case with him. If anyone called or rang up she was to say that he was out of Town—nothing more.

"Very well, Mr. Cosmo. But what about that Madame Luna if she comes?"

"Keep her here until I return."

"But if she won't stay?"

"I rely on your powers of persuasion."

Thor reached Lewes soon after noon and went first to the station. Apart from the constant stream of traffic that flows through the long narrow and tortuous High Street the quaint old town seemed quiet enough, drowsing placidly in the July sun on the hillside, crowned by the grey ruins of its castle overlooking the cornfields and pastures of the valley of the Ouse. Thor felt that on leaving the main road he left the twentieth century and went back to the days of his early youth. The reek of petrol was exchanged for the scent of syringa from some garden hidden behind high walls. A baker's cart drawn by an old brown horse creaked slowly by. Rooks cawed in the high elm trees. Outside the station an authentic growler, a perfect museum piece, with its horse munching the contents of his nosebag, stood in a line with two taxis and an outside porter who sat on his truck and eyed Thor's descent from his car without interest.

He brightened as Thor approached him. "Luggage, sir? I can fetch or carry to any part of the town."

"I've no luggage," Thor said, "but if you can help me with some information it'll be worth half a crown to you."

"I'll do my best, sir?"

"You are here every day?"

"Never miss except when I gets my bronchitis and my daughter won't let me go out."

"Can you remember last Friday week a small dark woman in a long brown tweed coat who arrived by one of the London trains? Don't say you do if you don't. That wouldn't help me at all."

The old man nodded. "Ah! I remember her right enough. It was plain to see she was in trouble. Eyes red with crying and all of a tremble. I was alone here on the rank, for the others all passengers up the hill, and she comes to me—" he broke off. "Look here, my telling you won't get her into no more trouble, will it?"

"No. I can promise you that. I'm a friend of hers."

The old man's clear blue eyes rested on Thor for a moment and seemed satisfied with what they saw, for he resumed. "She said, 'Can you tell me the way to Belgrave Manor?' I said, 'I don't know of no Belgrave Manor except over at Mitre Gap. You wouldn't want to go there. It's been standing empty dunnamany years,' and she said, 'That'll be the place. It's been taken. Is it far?' I said, 'It's six or seven miles. You couldn't walk it. Better wait for one of the taxis to come back to the rank to drive you over.' She said, 'I haven't the money for that. I'll have to walk.' I told her the way and off she went, but first she asked me about the trains back to London."

"You saw her again later?"

"No. And I was here when the up trains left until eight o'clock. I never saw her no more."

"I see," said Thor. "Thank you." He produced half a crown. "Where can I find out about this Belgrave Manor?"

The outside porter scratched his head reflectively. "At Garland's office they might tell you something. They're an old-established firm of house agents and auctioneers. I used to work for them. Mr. Garland's a nice gentleman and so's young Mr. Dennis. You go down the road towards Southover and you'll see a crescent of big old houses standing back from the road with a garden in front. The last house is theirs. They've got their office on the ground floor and live over same as Mr. Garland's father and grandfather did before him. Thank you, sir."

Thor got into his car and drove slowly along the road indicated. He soon came to the crescent of solid five-storied houses, built of red brick mellowed by the passing of two hundred years, and stopped where a brass plate on the door and wire blinds at the lower windows showed that a part of the premises was in use as an office. It was nearly one and a smell of roast mutton greeted him as he stepped over an old spaniel asleep on the mat, and turned the door handle. He found himself in a large cool hall with a glimpse of a sunny garden full of flowers through an open door at the far end. Another door on his right was marked OFFICE. PLEASE WALK IN. As he entered a young man in grey flannels who had been hammering the keys of a typewriter got up and came forward to meet him.

"What can I do for you?"

"I want to see Mr. Garland."

"I am Dennis Garland. Won't you sit down? Were you wanting a house in the neighbourhood?"

"There is a house called Belgrave Manor—"

"We have just let Belgrave Manor furnished as it stands for a year, but I daresay we have something else on our books that would suit you," said Dennis Garland briskly. "About how many rooms?"

"I'm sorry," said Thor, "I don't really need a house at present, but I had heard of the Manor—can you tell me the name of the present tenant?"

"It has been taken by a Mrs. Maulfry."

Thor had rather expected that. "I see," he said. "And she's staying there now? I know her slightly and might call—"

"She may be down any day now," said the young man. "I hope so anyway."

"May I ask why?"

"Well, Miss Kent's absolutely alone there with the little girl. They haven't even a woman to come in from the village."

"Who is Miss Kent?"

"Haven't you met her? She's the kid's governess, and she's awfully young herself. Only about nineteen. And the Manor's not the sort of place for a girl to be alone in. I think it's very plucky of her to stick it."

"Has she complained to you?"

"Oh, good Lord, no!" The young man reddened. "I've only just met her walking over the Downs, and we got talking. She says Mrs. Maulfry has been awfully kind to her. And she—Mrs. Maulfry—has got some notion of living a picnic existence and not being bothered with servants when she comes down to the country. Between you and me," said Dennis, becoming confidential, "I can't imagine why she took the place. It's been standing empty for donkey's years. The present owner is in New Zealand, and he never lived in it. His uncle died there. He was a bit eccentric, I fancy. I was away at school at the time. My father knows more about that than I do. Anyway, we tried to sell it but didn't get any bids, and there was some clause in the old man's will about not selling the furniture. We tried to find someone in the village to keep the place aired, but they won't go near it. So you can pretty well imagine the state it was in."

"I suppose Mrs. Maulfry has had it done up?"

"She hasn't. Barring sending down some beds and bedding and a lot of tinned provisions and having the water in the well analysed. It's this fad for camping out and roughing it, I suppose."

"No doubt," said Thor. "Well, I think I'll run over and make Miss Kent's acquaintance."

"You can't do that," said Dennis.

"Why not?"

"Well—the gate into the lane is padlocked. There's only the little door into the walled kitchen garden that opens on to the

Down at the back. Miss Kent has the key of that and has to lock and unlock it when she goes in and out. Mrs. Maulfry thinks it safer while she's alone there, in case of tramps, though there aren't any tramps so far off the main road."

"Dear me," said Thor, "well, do you think I could make the young lady's acquaintance as you did, more or less accidentally, by taking up a strategic position on the hill side?"

Dennis turned red again, looked at the older man doubtfully, and, seeing that he was smiling, grinned disarmingly.

"Oh, I've had to hang about a bit," he admitted, "she—she's worth it. Mind you, she's not one of these modern girls. She's different. Look here, sir, will you have a spot of lunch with us, and I'll go along with you?"

Thor accepted the invitation, and Dennis, after giving some instructions to a bespectacled young woman who emerged from an inner office to take his place at the typewriter, led the way upstairs.

Nothing had been changed in the Garlands' house since John Garland brought his young wife home. The solid mahogany furniture that had been good enough for his grandparents was good enough still. Mary Garland had been planning loose covers of flowered chintz and new wall papers, but she had been ailing throughout her short married life and had died when Dennis was born. Dennis had been at a boarding school during the four years of the War. When his father came home in 1918 with his D.S.O. and his stiff knee, he had brought with him his old batman, and the house thereafter had been womanless. Briggs did not shine as a housemaid, but he was an excellent cook, and Thor, as he entered the dining-room was greeted by a very savoury smell. John Garland, who had begun his lunch, got up from the table.

"Father, this is Mr.—"

"My name is Thor. Cosmo Thor."

"Mr. Thor knows Mrs. Maulfry, Father. Will you sit here, sir? Briggs is fetching another plate."

"I am most grateful for this hospitality," said Thor. He had liked the firm grip of John Garland's hand. His eyes were like his son's, very blue and rather round and child-like.

There was about them both an air of guileless simplicity that would make them the predestined prey of race-course touts and confidence men—but, if their business was prospering, as it seemed to be, they were probably not quite so unworldly as they appeared. Thor wasted no time in coming to the point.

"The little girl's mother came down to the Manor to see her about ten days ago, didn't she?"

"I don't think so," said young Garland, "Miss Kent would have told me."

"I can't say I care to think of those two being quite alone there," said his father.

"It's been empty some time, your son tells me."

"The Manor? Yes. Ever since old Wynyard died there. He left it to his nephew, but he's living in New Zealand. It has been on our books for years. We had quite given up hope of either letting or selling. I don't know how Mrs. Maulfry came to hear of it but I fancy it was through her friend, Mr. Quayle. It needs repair, but the owner won't spend any money on it. Mrs. Maulfry has only taken it for a year—but if you're a friend of hers I expect you know all about it."

"They wouldn't get servants to stay there," said young Garland.

"The place has a bad name?" asked Thor.

John Garland nodded. "It always had, I believe, since the days of the old Squire. He flourished towards the end of the seventeenth century. You can see his tomb in the churchyard of the old church on the hill. There's a whole crop of local legends, or there used to be. But you know a lot of smuggling went on along the Sussex coast and very likely some of the more blood-curdling yarns were invented by the owlers to keep the roads clear for themselves. The place changed hands about fifty years ago. The man who bought it, old Wynyard, was eccentric from the first. He shut himself up there. A queer fish. Lived alone with one man servant. He sent for me one day. Nineteen twelve I think it was. You were at school, Dennis. He'd had a stroke during the night and had lost the use of his hands and he couldn't speak plainly, but he managed to make his servant understand that I was to be fetched. He had a second stroke before I got there. He tried to tell me something but he couldn't get it out. A painful business. I tried to help by making suggestions but it was no use. The poor devil was crying. I don't care to think of it even now. We had to give it up. He died that night. When the nephew heard the place had been left to him he cabled to us to sell."

"The man servant couldn't help? He knew nothing of his master's wishes?" said Thor.

"No. Wynyard had left him a thousand pounds and his books—but the books were to be burnt. He made a bonfire of them in the yard. He left the neighbourhood and I don't know what became of him. You couldn't get much out of him, but he turned to me once after the funeral—he and I were the only mourners—and he said, 'It was a stroke—but what brought it on? If you ask me, sir, he died of fright.'"

"Dear me," said Thor, "that's very interesting. Very."

The roast mutton had been followed by redcurrant tart and cream. Briggs brought in the coffee and left the room.

"Mr. Thor is going over to see Miss Kent, Father. I thought, if you could spare me this afternoon, I could show him the way," said Dennis.

"Very well. If you'll go down to the office now and tell Miss Smith to let the printers have the catalogue of that sale on the 19th of next month. We must send them out in good time."

"All right. I'll do that."

When he had gone the elder Garland, who had been lighting his cigar, turned to Thor. "My son seems very interested in this Miss Kent," he remarked, "I have not met her myself. I must admit that I'm getting a bit worried. I wonder if you'd mind telling me—what sort of girl is she?"

"I've no idea. I never heard of her before your son mentioned her."

"I thought you were a friend of her employer—" began Garland.

"Hardly a friend. An acquaintance. I am chiefly concerned with the little girl—" He rose with some alacrity as Dennis put his head in at the door. He did not want to embark on further explanations just then.

"Cheerio!" The young man was in unconcealed high spirits. "I'll bring Mr. Thor back to tea, here. Tell Briggs we shall want a good spread. It's hungry work tramping over the Downs. Do I come with you, sir, or shall I lead the way on my motor cycle?"

Thor smiled. "I decline to follow one of those noisy horrors. You will come with me."

Thor did not talk at first. He was fully occupied in making his way through the congested traffic on the long High Street, but when they had left the town behind and were following the road eastward across the valley he broke the silence.

"Where do we park the car?"

"We must go through Mitre Gap—that's the village—and up the lane by the park wall of the Manor on to the open Down. We can't get any farther though there's a kind of sunken way like a ditch between banks and hedges right up to the old church. As a matter of fact I was going there anyhow this afternoon if I could wangle a couple of hours off," he added ingenuously. "She usually walks that way, and I sent a couple of chaps along to repair the church roof. We try to keep the outbuildings weather proof."

"Don't the churchwardens look after the church?"

"Not this one. It belongs to the estate and hasn't been used for public worship for over a century."

They had left the main road and turned to the right, following a bye road through a cleft in the bare green rampart of the chalk hills. They came presently to a few cottages strung out along the road side. "There's the parish church," said Dennis, indicating a grey Norman tower half hidden among trees. "That's the vicarage, and there's my cousin Millicent. Do you mind stopping? I'm relying on her to look after those two a bit."

Thor complied and a young woman who had just emerged from a cottage opposite the vicarage came up to them.

"Hallo, Den," she shouted. "Better late than never. You haven't been near us for ages."

Dennis introduced Thor and she proffered a limp hand, talking all the while to her cousin. She had red cheeks, hard brown eyes, a loud, over-bearing manner. "I've been parishing. You know what father is. He never goes near them. He wouldn't get a quorum if I didn't round them up." She laughed stridently. "Come in and I'll get the tea. It's Annie's afternoon out. Bring your friend—"

"Sorry we can't to-day, Millie. Another time. Has Miss Kent called?"

Millicent Gale's smile vanished. "If you mean the nursemaid with the child from the Manor they came yesterday. I couldn't think why."

"I told her to come. I said you'd be no end bucked to have another girl to talk to. You gave them tea, I hope," said Dennis.

"I did not. I just spoke to them at the door. Don't be an ass, Dennis. I shall call on this Mrs. Maulfry when she comes down, naturally. This girl you're making such an absurd fuss about is simply one of the servants. I'm not going to put myself in a false position by getting pally with her. Yes, I got your note about her."

"I see," the boy's face was white with anger. "And the founder of your religion was the son of the village carpenter. Funny. Damned funny."

"You need not be blasphemous," said his cousin coldly.

"All right. Will you drive on, Mr. Thor?"

"You might not think it," he said when they left the village behind them, "but Millie can be quite decent. I used to spend my holidays at the vicarage when father was in France. It's a dull life for her. My uncle is always buried in his books. I thought she'd jump at the chance of seeing something of another girl," he added ruefully.

Thor made no comment. Millicent Gale was not attractive, but he felt rather sorry for her.

They turned to the left up a lane skirting the eight foot wall that enclosed the estate. Thor noticed the spikes on the top.

"They're afraid of trespassers."

"That was old Wynyard, I believe. I've heard my father say he had a nervous horror of somebody getting in. No need to worry now. The village boys wouldn't come near the place. They used to come and shy stones through the iron entrance gates. We shall be passing them in a minute. But they got a fright, I believe, and they've given Belgrave a wide berth since then."

They passed the gates. Thor noted the padlock. Inside a weed grown drive wound away between huge overgrown banks of laurel. A quarter of a mile farther up the hill they emerged on the open Down and the track vanished abruptly in a bed of nettles. Thor turned the car before they got out. They walked half a mile along the bank crowned with hornbeams gnarled by the prevailing south-west winds. Their objective was visible on the hillside above and, at a distance, looked like a barn. To approach it they passed between two mouldering wooden posts that had once held a gate. Thor, following his companion, realised that the mounds hidden in the long grass over which he stumbled were forgotten graves.

They were approaching the building from the west. As they walked round to the north side Thor glanced up with a sudden uneasy feeling that something threatened from above and saw that one of the workmen was sitting astride on the roof and leaning down to grip the top of a long ladder set against the north wall. At the same instant there was a warning cry and the ladder slipped sideways and another man who was on it fell heavily.

Young Garland and Thor both hurried forward and helped him to his feet. He seemed dazed and blood was running from his wrist but otherwise he appeared unhurt.

He turned reproachfully to an older man standing by. "Why didn't you hold the ladder steady, Tom, like I asked you to."

"I did, but it was jerked away like. You're lucky it's no worse. We didn't ought to have come here. I wouldn't if I hadn't been out of a job so long."

Thor had torn his handkerchief into strips and was binding the cut on the other man's wrist. "It's more of a scrape than a cut." He saw a sharp-edged fragment of stone, recently broken and smeared with blood, lying among the nettles that grew in that sunless patch of ground under the north wall by a narrow arched doorway. "What is it?"

"The stone cross from the roof. It got blown off, or struck by lightning, may be, weeks ago. Mr. Dennis he told us to fix it up again with a brace like, but Tom Mills here said it warn't no manner of use."

"That's right," said Mills, "what's to be will be on Belgrave Down, and tain't no good interfering."

"How can you talk such rot, Tom," said young Garland, "you ought to know better at your age."

"Age hasn't nought to do with it," said Mills with the slow immovable obstinacy of his kind. "I knew no good would come of us messing about up here. If the old church is to fall let her fall. My mother lived at Mitre Gap till she was married and that's going back nigh seventy years. The children never came up here after cowslips, nor yet blackberrying in those days, and they don't now. What's more you won't find no rabbits' burrows hereabouts, nor no birds neither."

Dennis was bending to look at the broken bits of stone scattered about their feet. "Well, it's past mending now, anyway," he said. "Better leave it, I suppose. Did you borrow the ladder down the village?"

"Yes, sir. We can carry it back now," said Charlie, betraying some eagerness to leave the spot.

"That's all very well, but what about your wrist?"

"I can use my other hand, sir."

Old Mills was collecting the tools in a bag. He, too, was obviously in a hurry to be gone.

Thor was looking about him in a puzzled way. "What about the other chap?" he asked.

"Which other, sir?"

"The one who was sitting astride on the roof."

Mills' withered lips moved for an instant soundlessly. Then he said, "There was only me and Charlie. He was on the ladder and I was steadying it from the ground."

"I see," said Thor. "My mistake. It must have been an effect of light, an illusion. Queer, though. I could have sworn—"

Dennis was growing impatient. All this was delaying them. Miss Kent and her small pupil would be farther up the hill. He fancied he could see a moving patch of pale blue half a mile away on the ridge. The men had collected their tools. He saw them lift the ladder and trudge away.

"That's that," he said, relieved. "We've our duty to our client and we do what we can to keep the outbuildings in repair, but you see the difficulty."

They walked on together up the hill.

"What is the trouble exactly?" asked Thor.

"I'm hanged if I know. All the villagers go on like that fellow Mills. You might think he was a slacker, but he isn't. He's a good worker and takes a pride in finishing his job. I knew he didn't want to come here, but we can't let everything fall to pieces."

"But they won't say anything definite?"

"No. They're afraid of being laughed at, I suppose. If you ask a direct question they simply shut up. Of course there was a lot of smuggling about here in the old days, and some say it has started again. I sometimes wonder if that isn't the explanation. The old church would make a very good storehouse for stuff that has evaded the Customs."

"It's a possibility," said Thor, "an explanation. But I doubt if it covers all the facts. Is this Miss Kent?"

A girl who had been sitting on the turf in the shade of a clump of gorse got to her feet as they came towards her. She had brown hair and brown eyes, and she was, as Dennis had said, very young.

"Hallo!" said Dennis, "I say, I'm awfully glad we came this way. This is Mr. Thor."

"How do you do," she said. Though she was evidently almost as shy as Dennis himself she had an attractive smile. "Allie, where are you? She's collecting stones."

The little girl came round from the farther side of the gorse bushes. She appeared to be about five years old and was very pale and delicate-looking, with a tiny pointed face framed by soft little wisps of fair hair. She was carrying a large and knobbly flint in her grubby little paws and she showed it to them with great pride.

"Look what I found. Isn't it 'normous? May I keep it, Miss Kent, to give to Mummie?"

"It's rather heavy," said Celia Kent, smiling down at the earnest upturned face. "Are you sure Mummie will like it?"

From where they stood on the crest of the ridge they could see the roof and chimneys of the Manor embowered in a dense mass of trees and shrubberies in the valley below. The place looked dreary and dark even on a summer afternoon, and Thor did not wonder that Miss Kent spent as much time as possible away from it and wandering over the Downs.

"Look here," he said, "isn't there a place within walking distance where we could get tea?"

Dennis brightened. "There's Susan's Parlour. It's miles away by road but not far if you cut across the Downs. Come along, Miss Kent. I'll carry Allie if she gets tired. You'd love it, Allie. There'll be jam and cream."

Thus encouraged the party set out, walking quickly over the springy turf, while the larks sang overhead, and presently came down the other side of the hill to one of those cottages whose orchards have been converted into tea gardens. There were swings and a see-saw for children in an adjoining field, and at Thor's suggestion Dennis took Allie there, leaving Celia Kent with him sitting at a table in the shade of an apple tree.

"Garland tells me you're quite alone at the Manor with your pupil?"

"Yes. But Mrs. Maulfry may be down any day now. I don't mind really. She wants to do without servants and be quite free."

"I see." He was watching the shadows of the leaves of the apple tree on the pale blue linen of her frock. "Allie's mother came down to see her last week, didn't she?"

Celia shook her head. "No. Allie is always expecting her, but Mrs. Maulfry told me she had to go away and that she couldn't possibly be back until about the end of September."

"There might be some mistake about that," Thor suggested. "She may have come when you were out on the hills and gone away again."

Celia looked startled and uneasy. "Wouldn't she have written or something? Of course the gates are kept locked. She couldn't get in. But she would not come alone. Mrs. Maulfry would bring her."

"Of course," said Thor smoothly. The waitress had come up with a laden tea tray and Dennis and Allie were returning from the field. "Have you been with Mrs. Maulfry long?" he asked.

"Not quite a month. She engaged me to look after Allie. And she's been so kind."

"Your home is in London?"

"I haven't got a home. I'm quite alone since my mother died last year."

Allie came running up, her wan little face pink with unwonted excitement. "He swinged me. I went up ever so high."

There was jam and cream as Dennis prophesied and they all seemed to enjoy themselves. Dennis kept Allie in shrieks of laughter. Only Thor was rather silent, and if there had been anyone to observe him they might have fancied that he had something on his mind that worried him. It was he who looked at his watch presently. "It's nearly seven, and it will take at least an hour to climb the hill and go down the other side."

Celia looked startled. "I had no idea it was so late. Why, Allie, it's your bedtime. It's been lovely, but we must go at once."

The bill was paid and they started on the walk back. Allie was tired and inclined to be fretful, and Dennis carried her on his back.

"He's so good with her," Celia said to Thor, "she simply adores him. I hope Mrs. Maulfry won't mind our having had tea here," she said anxiously, "we're not allowed to go into the village. She heard there was a case of diphtheria."

Thor was silent for a moment. Then he said, "There was no harm in it, but if Mrs. Maulfry is inclined to be nervous about germs and so on perhaps you'd better not mention it."

She looked up at him uncertainly. "I—I don't want to be deceitful," she murmured.

Thor was silent for a moment. Then he said abruptly, "Do you ever rely on your instincts, Miss Kent?"

"I—I think so. Sometimes," she said. "Why?"

"Well—look at me. Do you feel that you can trust me?"

She looked up at him quickly. He met her eyes with the rare smile that transfigured the lean, harsh-featured face. Celia drew a long breath. "Yes," she said.

"Good. Then I shall ask you to do what I tell you without expecting explanations. There is something—but I'm in the dark, feeling my way. I am not going to ask anything of you at present." He realised that Mrs. Maulfry must inevitably hear of his coming through Allie's chatter. She had definitely assumed the sole responsibility for the child's welfare and she would almost certainly resent his interference. That was unfortunate, but it could not be helped. And, after all, she might recognise that they both had the same end in view. She must be as anxious as he was to solve the mystery of Madame Luna's death when once she became convinced, as he was, that the woman whose body had been found at the foot of the cliff in Devonshire was Allie's mother.

They had passed the spot where they had met earlier in the afternoon. The derelict church, away on the left, was huddled on the hill side like some small crouching animal in the gathering dusk. There was something animal, too, about the dense wood surrounding the Manor farther down the hill.

A humped furry back, thought Thor, and two chimneys like pricked ears. There was something deceptive he felt, in that immobility. It would hardly have surprised him at that moment if the whole dark mass had slid swiftly down into the valley as a water-vole on the bank of a stream slips into the water. They had reached the door in the high encircling wall of the kitchen garden. Celia produced her key. She had lost her high spirits and looked pale and tired. Allie was half asleep. Dennis set her gently on her feet. He had borne Thor's virtual monopoly of

Celia with commendable restraint, but as they shook hands he muttered, "I shall see you to-morrow?"

Celia tried to smile. "Perhaps."

The empty house awaited her with its empty rooms, its passages that echoed with every unaccustomed footfall, its doors that creaked gently when she woke in the night, without any apparent cause.

Thor may have read her thoughts. "Look here," he said as he gave the small fingers a reassuring grip. "If at any time you should need help—a friend—" He looked at Garland, whose response was instant and enthusiastic.

"Oh, rather! Send for me, Miss Kent, and I'll come like a shot at any time."

CHAPTER IV
SEBASTIAN QUAYLE

THOR drove to the Falcon, in the High Street, dropping Dennis Garland on his way. He had promised to go down to Southover later in the evening to have a talk with the father and son. He realised that if he wanted to retain the elder man as his ally he must admit him to his confidence to some extent at least. The boy would be less exacting. He was so obviously pledged to the service of Celia Kent in any case.

He booked a room and went into the coffee-room for dinner. The room, low pitched and panelled in wood blackened with age, was dark, and he did not at first notice his only fellow diner, seated at a table not far from his own. He had begun his fish when his attention was attracted.

"Waiter. Good God! waiter, do you call this coffee? Take the horrible stuff away and tell the cook that I shall make my coffee myself in future, in my own room, as I have done hitherto."

A beautiful voice and a beautiful enunciation, precise to the point of pedantry. A trifle affected, perhaps. An actor, thought Thor as he turned his head. No, not an actor. His fellow guest was Sebastian Quayle. There was no mistaking that short, fattish figure, a shade too sleek and well groomed, that pallid hairless face with its wide, lipless mouth and heavy-lidded, watchful eyes. Quayle was one of the few amateur collectors who could hold his own with the dealers. He had been pointed out to Thor at Christie's, where he was a well known figure. He was rich, unmarried, a great traveller, though his wanderings in the less civilized portions of the globe had not so far resulted in either a book or a film. He had not appeared to look in Thor's direction, but he stopped at his table on his way out.

"I am not a boy scout, but I am disposed to do one good deed. Don't touch the coffee here. A more noxious brew I never"—his eyes narrowed—"pardon me. You are Dr. Thor?"

"Not doctor—"

"Really not? Surely a degree of science? But the occult sciences are not recognised by our Universities, eh? I am delighted to meet you. My name, by the way, is Quayle."

He sat down, uninvited, in a chair facing Thor's across the table, and took a cigarette from a platinum case.

"I have these made for me. A very special blend."

"Doped?" said Thor bluntly.

Quayle waved a plump white hand. "A little. Nothing you have ever heard of. Not poppy nor mandragora. The average Elizabethan knew more of herbs than we do."

"But you know something?" suggested Thor.

The little man smirked. "A little. The subject has always interested me. I have a unique collection of old books containing some very curious recipes." He licked his lips. "Heaven or hell from a pinch of dust, a smear of ointment."

Thor, who had declined the meat course, was eating gooseberry tart. "You've tried them out?" he said. He sounded indifferent, but Quayle looked at him quickly and when he answered there was a subtle change in his manner.

"Not really. The ingredients are apt to be either too costly or too hard to come by. One does not take these things too seriously. My latest craze is bird watching. That is why I am often down here. The valley of the Ouse is ideal for my purpose. I spend happy hours wandering about with a pair of field glasses."

"I see," said Thor, "it must be most absorbing."

Quayle stood up. "It is. The billiard table here isn't too bad. What about a game?"

"Thanks," said Thor, "I have to go out to-night."

"You have friends in Lewes?"

"Yes."

"I'll say good night then," said Quayle, and drifted away.

The waiter rushed forward obsequiously to open the door for him.

Thor looked after him thoughtfully. Bird watching. It was difficult to imagine a man of Quayle's type taking up so harmless a hobby. And why was he so friendly? Thor looked at his watch. He was later than he had meant to be. He went out to his car which he had left in the yard of the inn. On second thoughts he told one of the men in the yard to garage her. He would walk. He turned down one of the narrow steep lanes leading down the hill and within ten minutes was being shown, by Briggs, into John Garland's study. Two firm hand grips, two pairs of child-like blue eyes, the comforting unambiguous clouds of ordinary Virginian tobacco. All these things were refreshing after even a short colloquy with Mr. Sebastian Quayle.

Thor declined the proffered whisky and soda.

"Dennis tells me you have decided to stay in Lewes for a bit," began John Garland. "I—may I be quite frank, Mr. Thor?"

"Yes, please."

"Well, my son says you met this Miss Kent and the little girl on Belgrave Down and took them out to tea. That's very nice, but I gather that it isn't all? I mean, you have some further object in view, haven't you? Mrs. Maulfry is our client. If she does not want any member of her household to meet with people in the neighbourhood that is her affair. To put it quite bluntly, I'm not sure that I approve of Dennis hanging about the Manor gates in the hope of meeting her governess. It's—damn it—it's undignified."

"I don't blame you," said Thor; "put that way it sounds an unpleasantly underhand proceeding. On the other hand if you had met Miss Celia Kent—I hope you will some day—I think you would agree with me that she is a thoroughly nice girl, simple and unspoilt. She is undoubtedly pretty, but I don't think I have allowed myself to be influenced by that fact. I am middle-aged and not at all susceptible. What struck me even more than her looks, Mr. Garland, was her youth, and another fact that I elicited in the course of conversation. She has no near relations, and, apparently, no friends. That's a hard case, but not uncommon in this hard world."

"It isn't going to help her to put her in the wrong with her employer," said Garland.

"If you ask me," said Dennis suddenly and explosively, "the sooner she gets another job the better."

"Does she complain of Mrs. Maulfry's treatment of her?" asked his father.

"No. No, I can't say she does."

Garland turned again to Thor. "You didn't know of Miss Kent's existence, did you, when you came to us this morning?"

Thor smiled appreciatively. Certainly those round blue eyes were not as child-like as they seemed. "Quite right," he said. "I didn't. I'll tell you now why I came to Lewes."

He told them everything, beginning with his meeting with Madame Luna in the train running into Euston. When he had done there was a silence. Dennis broke it. His boyish face was unusually grave.

"Do you really mean that this woman was Allie's mother, and that she was murdered?"

"I have no proof," said Thor, "but that is what I believe." Garland was frowning. "Wait a bit. She called at your flat on the Friday morning and you were gone. She then went to Mrs. Maulfry, still in the state of hysterical distress described by your housekeeper. Mrs. Maulfry promised to look after the little girl, advised her to have a few weeks' rest in some quiet seaside place, and gave her some money to go on with. Mrs. Maulfry has not heard from her since and neither have you, but a woman's body was found at the foot of Barme Head the following Monday, and when you went down there, too late to see her, you found the unused half of a return ticket from London to Lewes in the bushes a few feet from the spot where she probably fell over. You are building a good deal on that ticket, aren't you?"

"More than that," said Thor. "I got a pretty good description from the luggage porter outside the station here. She came to Lewes and enquired the way to Belgrave Manor. We can assume that she wanted to see her little girl. Natural enough. But there the thread breaks."

Garland drew at his pipe. "What does Mrs. Maulfry think? You say you called on her yesterday?"

"She pointed out that there was no actual identification of the body found at the foot of the cliff. She is still hoping that Madame Luna will turn up again. If she doesn't she is prepared to adopt the child."

"Well, that's satisfactory," said Garland, "she's a good sort evidently, even if she is a bit eccentric. The little girl is well cared for. Can't you leave it at that, Mr. Thor? If the mother turns up, well and good. If she doesn't the child may have a better chance in life than she would have done. There's something to be said for a fairy godmother."

"Perhaps," said Thor, "but I'd like to know how Madame Luna got from here to Barme Head."

"She need not return to Victoria," argued Garland, "she could go to Brighton and get a train from there to Salisbury and change there."

"Yes," said Thor, "but why did she say 'My God!' and burst out crying when my housekeeper told her I was out. She had quarrelled with her landlady and she was worried over the future. She thought the police would stop her from earning her living as a palmist. But there must have been something more. I've got to find out what it is."

"If you agree that she may have gone down to Devonshire the way I suggested everything falls into place," said Garland. "She walked to Belgrave Manor, found the gate padlocked and assumed that the little girl had been taken back to London. She tramped back to Lewes. She may have gone on to Brighton by bus. She carried out the plan suggested to her of going to a little seaside village. Perhaps she knew the place and hoped to get lodgings at the coastguard's cottages along the cliff. There was a sea fog and she went too near the edge."

"Yes," said Thor.

Dennis Garland was watching him. "You'd like to believe that?" he said.

Thor nodded. "I'd like to," he agreed. He glanced at the clock on the mantelpiece and exclaimed, "I'd no idea it was so late. I'm keeping you up. I must thank you for listening to me so patiently. I can rely on your discretion, of course. This will go no further?"

"You can rely on us."

Briggs had gone to bed. Dennis went downstairs with him to the front door. "Look here," he said, "you mustn't mind my father. I know you still think there's some crooked business going on. If you need help and I can be of any use, I'm here, see?"

As he came out on the doorstep the old spaniel who had followed at his heels began to growl. He stooped to hold her by the collar.

"She goes for prowling cats," he explained, "and she's not a match for them. Good night."

"Good night," said Thor.

Was there a shadowy figure standing half hidden by the pillars of the portico of the adjoining house?

He fancied that there was, though he could not be sure and he did not choose to look more closely. As he walked back up the hill through the narrow moonlit streets he glanced back now and then but failed to see if he was followed.

At the Falcon he had been given a bedroom at the back of the house with a window looking towards the grey ruins of the castle soaring magnificently against the sky. He locked his door before he switched out the light and got into bed.

He slept late and did not get down to breakfast until past nine. Rather to his relief he saw that Quayle had been down before him and had gone out. There was, to his mind, something faintly nauseating about that plump and pallid personage. He was helping himself to marmalade when he was called to the telephone. He had rung up his housekeeper the night before and he expected to hear her voice, but though it was a woman speaking he realised at once that it was not Mrs. Jeal.

"Mr. Thor? Sebastian told me you were staying at the Falcon. Why didn't you tell me you'd like to see Allie? I should have been delighted to bring you down with me. What? Rina Maulfry speaking. That's why you've gone down to Lewes, isn't it? Quite. I'm coming down to-day and bringing some friends. Yes, Sebastian will be joining us. He's such a help to me. Will you lunch with us? Yet, at the Manor. To-day. A sort of picnic. I'm bringing food from Fortnum and Mason's. You will? Good."

Thor hung up the receiver and went back to his interrupted meal. Were his suspicions, his very vague suspicions, of Mrs. Maulfry's good faith unfounded? He told himself that they must be. A rich woman, charitable, kind-hearted. The typical fairy godmother of romance. Celia Kent, if she was a little in awe of her employer, had been eager in her praise of her unvarying kindness both to her and little Allie. As to Quayle, the little man was harmless enough, no doubt, if one could get used to his affectations.

When he left the dining-room there was no one in the hall or the telephone booth. He took the opportunity to ring up the Garlands, and to tell Dennis, who answered, that he was lunching at the Manor. "I'll come and see you later," he promised.

As he left the booth he found Quayle waiting to enter it. The little man greeted him with his expansive smile.

"You've heard from Rina? I happened to mention you were here when I rang her up last night. She has asked you to lunch? Splendid. Can I drive you over? Oh, you have your own car. You know the way? Rina will be charmed that you can come. She has heard so much about you and wanted to see more of you. But you have the reputation of a recluse."

"I haven't much time for dining out," said Thor.

"You don't like to be bored," said Quayle. "Neither do I. The hearty he-men. The red-faced raw-boned women who play golf or tennis. But Rina chooses her friends with the utmost care. The result is—interesting. Well, we shall meet again later."

Thor made way for him to go into the booth. "Did you do any bird watching last night?"

"A little," said Sebastian Quayle blandly. "The habits of most nocturnal birds are of extraordinary interest. Good-bye for the present."

CHAPTER V
LUNCH AT THE MANOR

THOR spent the rest of the morning on a seat in the castle grounds. He felt unusually depressed and curiously disinclined for any exertion. There was so little to go upon. His mind seemed to be full of wheels spinning uselessly in a void. John Garland's exposition of what had probably happened seemed to cover all the facts known to him. It accounted for Madame Luna's movements on the last day of her life; for the unused return ticket, for the fall over the edge of the cliff. He would have to make enquiries at Brighton station and at Salisbury. If he could find a porter or ticket collector who remembered her he would be satisfied. Only deep down in his subconscious something stirred uneasily, and, when he looked at his watch, it was almost as if a detaining hand had been laid on his arm.

Half-past twelve. It was time to start. He went back to the Falcon and got out his little two-seater car. He took the road he had followed the day before with Dennis Garland. As before he passed through the hamlet of Mitre Gap, where the only living things he saw were a cow looking over a gate and a cat asleep on a cottage window sill, and drove up the narrow rutted lane that led to the Manor. This time the entrance gate stood invitingly open. The weed-grown drive wound between high banks crowned with a dense growth of laurel. The house when he saw it was very much what he had expected. The original building had been overlaid with stucco and pseudo classic additions in the worst taste of the eighteenth century, and it showed traces of long neglect. The farther end of the long, two storied structure was smothered with ivy that had reached the roof and covered one chimney stack, the stucco on the walls was peeling off, the paint on the window frames blistered with age. Against this background the swarthy-faced chauffeur in the smart uniform who opened the car door seemed an incongruous figure. Apparently he was the only servant on the premises for, murmuring, "will you step this way," he ushered Thor into a circular hall lit by a lanthorn in the roof and surrounded by a gallery supported by pillars stuccoed in Pompeian red, and reached by a flight of stairs on the right. Thor had only time to note that the floor of black and white tiles was still crusted with the accumulated dust of years when one of the numerous doors opened and Mrs. Maulfry came towards him.

She was wearing a dress of a brown silk material with black spots and long gold earrings dangled from her ears. Thor thought he had seen faces like hers peering from under the canvas of gipsies' tilt carts. She did not offer her hand, but the brilliant black eyes in the ravaged face flashed a greeting.

"Welcome to my anchorite's cell," she said gaily. "I have lived in crowds and longed for solitude. Sebastian found this for me. Isn't it delicious?"

Thor glanced round the dim, musty-smelling hall. "It's certainly unusual," he said.

"You don't like it?" she said laughing. "You think it is florid, in bad taste. These red painted pillars, eh? I find them so amusing. We shall play hide and seek here when there are enough of us. The blind man in the middle where you are standing, where it is light. The others behind the pillars, under the gallery, in the shadow. In and out—" she ended on a chanting note and checked herself with her bony fingers laden with diamonds pressed to her lips.

"I see," he said. He still felt heavy and unhappily conscious of some lack of clearness in his mind. He had to make an effort to follow what she was saying.

"Why didn't you tell me you would like to see little Allie when you called the day before yesterday? You could have come down with me and saved yourself trouble and fatigue. You didn't really think I should mind?" She turned her head and raised her voice. "Miss Kent. Bring Allie here to say how do you do to Mr. Thor before you start."

Celia Kent came out of one of the rooms, leading the little girl by the hand.

"Miss Kent tells me you were kind enough to take them to tea somewhere," said Mrs. Maulfry negligently. "I'm sure they both enjoyed it. They are having another picnic to-day, but farther off. Manuel is taking them for a drive in the car. Run along, my dear. Be a good girl, Allie, and do what Miss Kent tells you."

The fairy godmother to the life, thought Thor. It was not difficult to imagine her turning a pumpkin into a Rolls Royce for her young protégées. He shook hands gravely with Celia and held Allie's fragile little paw in his firm grasp for a moment. He had no chance to say a word to Celia unheard by her patroness. He had to let them go. Manuel had brought the car round to the door and was waiting, with a rug over his arm.

"He'll take such care of them," said Mrs. Maulfry. "He has been with me for years."

"You brought him with you from South America?" hazarded Thor.

"Yes. But the others will be getting impatient. Come to lunch."

He followed her into a large gloomy dining-room where four people awaited them. Mrs. Maulfry introduced them all.

"Mr. Sebastian Quayle, one of my oldest and dearest friends. Lady Sabina Romaine, Miss Brenda Heriot, Dr. Streete."

Thor knew Lady Sabina by name and had seen her picture often enough in the papers. She had been much photographed at one time, first as the loveliest debutante of the year; then, after the spectacular scandal that led to her first appearance in the divorce court. After a brief career on the stage she had run a hat shop for a few months. There had been two more matrimonial experiments. The last husband, Colonel Romaine, the explorer and archaeologist, was somewhere in the upper reaches of the Amazon.

Lady Sabina was tall, exquisitely fair, thin to the point of emaciation. She reminded her admirers of ice and moonlight. It was soon evident that neither Quayle nor Streete could keep his eyes off her for long. Her movements were slow and languid, and she seldom troubled to speak. She was wearing a white sleeve-less frock, and a coat with a white fur collar hung over the back of her chair. Brenda Heriot was a middle-aged woman with a coarse, clever face, grey hair cut in an Eton crop, and a sharp, restless, impatient manner that suggested nerves under imper-fect control. Her name, too, was familiar. Thor remembered after a while where he had seen it. She was a sculptress and had been having a show of her work in Bond Street. Dr. Streete was lean, wiry, definitely shop-soiled in spite of his comparative youth and positive good looks. His eyes, meeting Thor's defiantly, were hard, and his mouth had a bitter twist. Thor had placed him too before lunch was over. A specialist in nervous diseases, practis-ing in Harley Street, assured of a brilliant future, he had been broken by the National Medical Council after the death of his reception secretary, a young and attractive girl, under circum-stances that had led to his being censured by the coroner. There had not been sufficient evidence for the police to act upon and the public had heard nothing more of the matter.

Though none of his companions were to his taste, Thor found himself enjoying his lunch. The food was excellent. There was no service. Quayle and the doctor got up to change the plates. All except Lady Sabina were good talkers. Their main subject, perhaps in deference to Thor's known interest in psychic science, was occultism. Miss Heriot summed up their attitude.

"I get a kick out of it," she said.

Quayle said, "Funny things happen. I was on a walking tour years ago in the Pyrenees. I had spent a night at an inn at the foot of a pass. It was about this time of year, and of course there wasn't the least danger from wolves at that season. Neverthe-less the people at the inn warned me that I might be followed through the woods by a wolf. They begged me not to shoot it. They knew I carried a revolver. They made such a point of it, especially the daughter, who was a very handsome girl, that I promised not to fire at the animal unless it attacked me. They thanked me profusely and I went my way. Before long I heard him coming after me. I glanced round and caught a glimpse of him. I must admit I got a shock. He was nearly twice the size of the average European wolf, who isn't much bigger than an Alsatian. But he kept his distance. He was after me all that day and only vanished when I was in sight of the next village on the other side of the pass. Frankly, I wouldn't care to take that walk again. The people where I stayed that night didn't want to talk about it, but I induced a fellow I hired as a guide the next day to give me his version. According to him the wolf was the lover of the innkeeper's daughter, a *loup garou*. Being a very jealous person he made a habit of spying on and following any traveller who spent a night at the inn. Fortunately for me," added Quayle with a smirk, "I had not paid any particular attention to his young woman."

"How marvellous!" murmured Lady Sabina. "Why don't I live in the Pyrenees?"

"A fearful place," quoted Quayle, looking at her.

> "As lonely and enchanted,
> As e'er beneath a waning moon was haunted
> By woman wailing for her demon lover."

Streete turned to Thor. "Have you dealt with any cases of lycanthropy?" he enquired.

"I had one," said Thor gravely.

"Do tell us about it," said Mrs. Maulfry.

He shook his head. "You wouldn't expect Dr. Streete to discuss his patients." The words were out of his mouth before he realised what a gaffe he had made. An apology would only make matters worse. He hurried on. "We don't know yet how far mind can work on matter. Autosuggestion. But when the change is unconscious, taking place during the sleep of the subject, it is more difficult to explain." He had been speaking at random, hoping to pass off an awkward moment, but Streete was not going to let either of them off so easily.

"Your reference to medical etiquette was unfortunate," he said harshly, "but perhaps you didn't know I'd been kicked out for unprofessional conduct. I have no patients now."

"Never mind, Hugh," said Miss Heriot, "you are well rid of their ridiculous red tape. You can pursue knowledge now in your own way."

Quayle was preparing the coffee at a side table. Thor could not see him without turning his head but he heard the liquid bubbling in its receptacle and the tinkling of the silver spoon stirring the grounds.

Brenda Heriot had lit a cigar and was puffing at it with an air of sensual satisfaction, her clumsy figure sprawling ungracefully in the chair she had pushed back from the table. Thor was trying to remember what the critics had said about her show. She specialised in small bronze groups of a somewhat ambiguous nature. Thor found himself watching her powerful sculptor's hands with their spatulate fingers and supple thumbs with a kind of reluctant admiration. It would be interesting, he knew, to see them at work on a lump of clay. But in spite of their strength they were restless. All these people, he realised, were suffering from nerves. As the minutes passed they were more and more on edge. Mrs. Maulfry's eyelids were twitching. Lady Sabina, who had been arranging her face with the aid of a little mirror, closed her bag and sat looking at him. They were all waiting, Thor felt, for something to happen. The rather airless room was filled with the rich aroma of coffee.

Quayle filled the tiny yellow cups and brought them round to his fellow guests. When he came to Thor the latter shook his head. "No, thanks. No coffee." He noticed that Quayle did not set his cup down before one of the others but carried it back to the tray.

Mrs. Maulfry broke a silence that had lasted barely a minute, though to them all it had seemed much longer.

"Oh, by the way, Mr. Thor, you will be interested to hear that I have had a letter from Madame Luna. It came last night. She has been staying in the country, as I advised, and is feeling much better already."

"I am delighted to hear it," he said. "Might I see the letter?"

Her eyebrows went up. "Really, Mr. Thor. One would almost think you doubted my word."

"Oh, surely not," he said with a smile, "just a natural curiosity. She came to my flat in such distress. I want to know why."

"She makes no reference to you," said Mrs. Maulfry. And now her black eyes glittered and her tone was openly inimical. Thor realised that with every moment that passed his position was more untenable, but he persisted.

"Nevertheless I should like to see it."

"Would you know her handwriting?"

"I think so."

"I am sorry," she said. "I left the letter in London."

Thor got to his feet. "I am afraid I must be going," he said.

Quayle and the doctor exchanged glances and the latter got up.

"Mrs. Maulfry has had the stables turned into a garage of sorts. I'll take you round."

They went out through the hall which, with its circle of red painted pillars, looked more like the deserted temple of some tawdry and sinister eastern god than the entrance to an English country house, and round the corner to the arched entrance to the stable yard.

"If you'll wait here," said Streete uneasily, "I'll see where Manuel has put your car. He would have to move her out of the way before he got out the Rolls."

"Very well," said Thor. He might have said, "I'll come with you," but he knew by this time that it would come to the same thing in the end. He glanced about him as Streete left him and saw that he would not be overlooked from the house. Streete was away for two or three minutes. When he returned Thor was stooping to retie a shoelace.

"I'm awfully sorry," said Streete more civilly than he had yet spoken, "Manuel is an ass. There are three lock up garages. He has run yours in to the end one and gone off with the key. A perfectly idiotic thing to do. I'm afraid it means that you'll have to wait here until he brings Miss Kent and Allie back from their drive. Too bad. I expect you feel you've had quite enough of our society." He took Thor's arm and led him unresisting, round towards the front of the house. The laurels met over their heads.

Underfoot there was a thick carpet of dead leaves. A dark and sunless path. Thor said nothing. He was thinking, "Well, I'm past fifty. I've had a good innings."

Something rustled just behind them. Streete let go of Thor's arm and leapt aside.

CHAPTER VI
DENNIS IS DISAPPOINTED

JOHN Garland glanced up from his book as his son jumped up for the tenth time and went over to the window. This was the hour before bedtime when the elder man liked to be quiet and undisturbed. "Can't you settle to anything?" he enquired.

Dennis, who had been drumming on the window sill, turned to face him. "He said he'd come round after being to the Manor. Why hasn't he? You're sure he didn't while I was out this afternoon?"

"Quite sure. Why don't you ring up the Falcon and find out if he's there?"

"He asked me last night not to do that."

His father grunted disapprovingly. "I don't like these mysteries. What is it all about? What is he driving at? If there's anything wrong the police are there. What do we pay rates for?"

"I don't understand any more than you do," said his son, "but I do feel that if Mr. Thor is worried there's something to worry about."

Garland closed his book, keeping his finger in the page he had been reading. "I see we'll have to thresh this out," he said. "This man seems to have made a great impression on you, Dennis. How long have you known him?"

"Since yesterday morning. But what has that to do with it? If you can't tell he's straight, Father, you're no judge of character."

John Garland laughed. "All right. I admit I like him, too. But I don't want you mixed up in any sort of unpleasantness. Why should you be involved in a search for a woman who is a complete stranger? I don't feel at all happy about it, Dennis."

The young man did not answer at once. He stood by the open window looking out into the quiet night. A moth, attracted by the light of Garland's reading lamp, fluttered helplessly against the tilted shade.

"Father, don't you see?" He spoke without turning his head. "I've got to be mixed up in it as long as Celia Kent is there."

Garland put his book down and reached for his tobacco pouch, noticing as he did so that his hand was not quite steady. He glanced up wistfully at the pastel drawing of Mary Garland over the mantelpiece. If only the boy's mother had lived, he thought. "You mean—you are in earnest about this girl?"

"Yes, Father."

"That alters the case," said Garland. "If you are sure—"

"I'm quite sure."

"Then you must go ahead," said his father, "and do what you think right. It certainly is odd that you haven't heard anything more since this morning. Unless, of course, he's had some news of this woman that has recalled him to London. You may get a letter from him in the morning to tell you that the whole thing has been satisfactorily cleared up."

"I hope it may be that," said Dennis, "but meanwhile I've half a mind to walk up to the Falcon. I've got a good excuse. One of Twemlow's tenants in Mill Terrace wants a new rainwater butt and I promised I'd see the landlord about it."

"Very well," said Garland.

He sighed and then he smiled as he heard the boy run down the stairs and bang the front door. He was too young to bear suspense patiently.

He read, or tried to read for an hour, but he was listening all the while for his son's return. He got up as he heard Dennis taking the stairs two at a time, and was mixing himself a whisky and soda when he burst into the room.

"You were right, Father. He's gone back to Town."

"Well—that's all right, I suppose?"

"I suppose so," said Dennis doubtfully, "but Twemlow seemed rather surprised. He didn't settle his bill in the usual way with Mrs. Twemlow at the office. The maid who took hot water to his room before dinner found a note for Twemlow on the dressing-table. It just said he was leaving and enclosed five one pound notes, anything left over from the bill to be distributed to the staff. That was O.K. according to Twemlow, but rather abrupt. Of course he only had a small suit-case with him. What I don't understand is this. He rang me up this morning not so long before he started off to lunch at the Manor. He hadn't arranged to leave then. He said quite definitely that he would come round here later in the day. Why didn't he ring up again when he changed his plans? He must have known I'd be expecting him."

"You'll hear to-morrow," said his father. "Go to bed now."

Garland was shaving the next morning when he heard the series of knocks that heralded the postman making his way round the Crescent. He also heard Dennis, who had evidently got up earlier than usual, running down to get the letters as they cascaded through the slit in the door on to the mat, and something about his returning footsteps indicated that there had been no letter from Thor.

He was in the dining-room when his father entered, hastily devouring eggs and bacon.

"He hasn't written. Look here, Father, I've been thinking. Now Mrs. Maulfry has come down to the Manor can't I go over and ask her if she's satisfied, or if there are any outside repairs we can put through? After all, she's a new tenant and we represent the landlord. Neither you nor I have ever set eyes on her. It's not very satisfactory."

"We have had her cheque for the first three months' rent," his father reminded him, "and forwarded the money to Wynyard, minus our commission. It isn't usual to run after tenants to ask them if they want repairs done. Still, as an excuse it might just hold water. I confess to some curiosity about the lady myself. Her taste in country houses is unusual. Your—Miss Kent speaks well of her?"

"Oh, yes. She says she's most generous and kind. But I think she's a little afraid of her."

"When did you think of going?"

"This morning."

"I would wait until this afternoon if I were you," said Garland. "That will give Thor a chance to ring up. Incidentally, we are supposed to be a firm of auctioneers and estate agents and this is my day for Steyning. I'm afraid you'll have to carry on here while I'm gone. I'll try to be back by two."

"Oh—all right," said Dennis resignedly. "I'd forgotten Steyning."

Garland chuckled. "You've certainly got it badly."

Dennis cheated his impatience by cramming three mornings' work in to one, to the bewilderment of Miss Smith, the bespectacled young woman in the office, who was not used to such intensive methods. There was one trunk call from a prospective tenant of a house on the Brighton Road, but nothing from Thor. Usually on the days when Garland went to Steyning lunch was served an hour later, but this morning Dennis told Briggs to give him something on a tray, and Garland was hardly in the house when he was out of it. His motor cycle was ready and waiting by the kerb. "Perhaps on the way back," he thought, "I'll stop at the vicarage and make it up with poor old Millie. She can't help her rotten temper. She can be pretty decent." He remembered the time when he had had some childish complaint during one of the school holidays he had spent with his uncle and cousin during the War, while his father was in France. He was about ten then and Emily only fifteen, but she had sat up with him night after night.

Mitre Gap, as usual, seemed deserted when he flashed through it. When he turned up the lane and reached the entrance gates he received his first shock.

He had expected, since Mrs. Maulfry had arrived, to find them open, but they were securely fastened as before with a padlock and chain. He had dismounted and was standing there uncertainly when the man who had acted throughout as Mrs. Maulfry's intermediary came leisurely down the drive towards him.

"This is a private road," he began, "there is no way on to the Downs"—and then—"Dear me! It's young Garland, isn't it? I didn't recognise you for a moment. Are you wanting anything?"

"Well, I just thought I'd like to see Mrs. Maulfry and make sure she is satisfied."

"Oh, quite, I believe," said Sebastian Quayle. "She's resting just now, or I'm sure she'd be delighted to see you. She won't be always here, you know. Just now and then. I'll tell her you called to enquire. She'll let you know, I expect, if she wants anything done."

They looked at each other through the bars of the gate. Quayle was smiling broadly, but it was a smile that did not reach his eyes. Dennis was flushed but determined.

"How is Miss Kent?" he asked. "I—I've met her sometimes walking over the Downs. It's been lonely for her. I thought perhaps Mrs. Maulfry would let her and the little girl come to tea at the vicarage some day. The vicar is my uncle—" He had not meant to say that, but he would fix it, he thought.

He would make Millie be civil, and when she got to know Celia she could not help liking her.

"That's charming of you," said Quayle with even more than his usual graciousness. "I'm sure Mrs. Maulfry could make no objection, though I believe she has put the village out of bounds for fear of infection. But she agrees with you that it is rather lonely here and she has decided that Miss Kent and her little pupil shall remain here no longer."

Dennis made a not very successful effort to conceal his dismay.

"She—they're going?"

"They went this morning. Mrs. Quayle did not think either of them were looking well."

"Back to London?" said Dennis.

"I really couldn't say. I didn't ask. It is no business of mine. There is some talk of a cruise. But I must not keep you," said Quayle. "Very good of you to come. Good afternoon."

He nodded and went back as he had come round the bend of the drive.

Dennis remounted his motor cycle and rode home. He did not stop at the vicarage. He was in no mood to submit to being chaffed by his cousin on what he knew she would call his latest pash. And there was no need to try to enlist her sympathies for Celia now. She was gone. Well—he could write to her, couldn't he? They had Mrs. Maulfry's London address. A letter sent there would reach her. He was comparatively cheerful when he reached home, but his spirits were dashed again by his father's reception of his news.

"Why the devil do they keep the gate locked now that Mrs. Maulfry's there? It looks fishy," he grumbled.

"And I can't stick Quayle," said Dennis. "There's something slimy about that chap. He's too darned civil. Grinning away like the Cheshire cat."

"I suppose you couldn't ask him if Thor had gone back to Town?"

"I didn't get the chance. Besides, I don't think Thor wanted them to know I was in with him. I tell you what, Father. I'll write to Celia Kent this evening, and I'll write to Thor too. Then we shall have done all we can, and we'll just have to wait."

"I agree," said Garland, after a moment's consideration. "I wouldn't worry, my boy. It's all to the good that Miss Kent has left that house. She may be farther off but, in your place, I'd rather think of her almost anywhere than under that roof." Dennis looked uneasily at his father.

"I didn't know you felt so strongly about the place."

"Well, for years I've hardly thought of it," Garland said. "I never imagined we'd find a tenant for it. I'm beginning to wish we hadn't. It has brought back to my mind the night I went there when old Wynyard was dying and I stood by, helpless, while he struggled to speak. There are things in most men's lives that they would like to forget if they could. There's some dark secret connected with that house, Dennis. I'm sure of it," he said gravely.

"You never told me all this before," cried Dennis.

"I thought the less said the better."

"But what kind of secret?" persisted the young man.

Garland shrugged his shoulders. "There you have me. I haven't the least idea." He broke off as Miss Smith, who had been typing in the outer office, knocked at the door.

"It's gone six, please, Mr. Garland. Are there any more letters I can post on my way home?"

Dennis answered. "All right, Miss Smith. I'll be going out to the pillar box myself presently."

CHAPTER VII
BUSMAN'S HOLIDAY

"JUST off the boat train at Victoria, eh?" said Superintendent Cardew. "Well, there are bouquets for you from the Hamburg police and the Paris Sûreté. You seem to have a knack with foreigners, Collier."

Collier grinned. He had come straight to the Superintendent's room at the Yard to hand in his report. Another knack, that of being able to sleep at any time and under almost any conditions, accounted for his fresh and spruce appearance after a tedious night journey.

"Had a good crossing?"

"Rotten for the time of year."

His senior eyed him enviously. "Seemed to agree with you," he growled. "You don't want a holiday. Or do you?"

"I'd be glad of a few days," said Collier.

"All right. Take them. Report for duty a week from now."

"Thank you, sir."

Collier left the building, greeting friends on the way. The holiday was welcome, but unexpected, and he had made no plans. It was pleasant on the Embankment. The river sparkled in the sunlight, and a fresh breeze blowing up from the sea across the Essex marshes was stirring the leaves of the planes.

A nursemaid pushing a perambulator glanced invitingly at the sunburned young man in the well-cut grey flannels. He smiled back at her—she was a pretty girl—but he walked on. He had decided to take his suit-case back to his lodgings and to call on Thor on his way. He caught a Victoria bus at the entrance to Westminster Square and within ten minutes was entering the block of flats off Vincent Square. The porter, who knew him by sight as a friend of Thor's, was polishing the brass work in the vestibule. He touched his cap.

"I suppose you've heard, sir?"

Collier stopped. "Heard what?"

"About Mr. Thor's accident. It was in the papers. He must have skidded or something and run his car up against a tree. On a little used bye-road it was, near Edenbridge. Seems as if he missed his way. A lorry driver found him. The car was burning but he'd managed to crawl clear. He was conscious and he begged the man to take him along to London. So the chap, who knew a bit about first aid, bandaged him up a bit, and laid him on a heap of empty sacks and took him along, but when he got to Croydon he got the wind up proper. He'd been slowing down at intervals and shouting 'Are you all right?' and the poor gentleman had answered, but this time he didn't. The driver thought, 'If he's conked out who's to prove it wasn't me done him in?' So he spoke to the next policeman he saw, and the end of it was they took him to a nursing home near by, and there he lies, between life and death, as you might say." The porter paused for breath.

"How do you know all this?" asked Collier.

"The driver came along here, see? Mr. Thor had given him his address. 'Take me home,' he said. So the driver came along as soon as he'd delivered his load, thinking there might be a wife, see? Well, I saw him first, and then I took him up to tell the housekeeper. She left at once for Croydon and she isn't back yet."

"Can you give me the address of the nursing home?"

"I got it written down."

"Thanks. May I use your telephone?"

The porter hesitated. "Well—the landlord is rather particular about that."

"Never mind," said Collier. "On second thoughts, I'll go myself. Thank you."

Half a crown changed hands. The porter offered to call a taxi, but Collier was in a hurry. He dashed round the corner and was boarding a tram in the Vauxhall Bridge Road. Four minutes later he was getting into a train as it moved out of the station. He sank back on the cushions of an empty first class compartment and took a cigarette from his case. There was time now to think. Thor badly injured, perhaps dying. It was a blow. Collier, a hard worker, absorbed in his profession, giving it all his energies, had not many friends. He realised, with a pang, how much he would miss Thor's sympathy and understanding.

He got out at West Croydon and took a taxi to the address given him. A young nurse opened the door and he was shown into a small waiting-room. After what seemed a long time, but was actually only ten minutes, an older nurse bustled in with the factitious cheerfulness of her kind.

"You are a friend of Mr. Thor?"

"Yes. Can I see him?"

"I am afraid not. He is very ill. He has not regained consciousness."

"He was conscious at first?"

"So I heard from the lorry driver who picked him up on the road. But he was not conscious when he was brought here."

"When will he come round? Have you any idea?"

"Not yet, I am afraid. Perhaps—"

He looked at her. "Were you going to say perhaps never?"

"He is very ill," she repeated, "suffering from concussion. His housekeeper is here, sitting in the passage outside the door of the room in which he lies. I gather she is an old family servant and very devoted. There are hours for visitors, but we have stretched a point in her case. If you call again to-morrow afternoon you may be able to see him."

She stood up to indicate that the interview was at an end, but Collier did not take the hint.

"Will you ask her to come down here for a word with me?" he said. Unconsciously he used his official tone. The matron was quick to recognise the note of authority.

"Very well," she said.

She left him. Collier walked restlessly up and down the little room until the door opened again and Mrs. Jeal came in.

The old housekeeper's eyes were swollen with crying.

"Oh, Mr. Collier, sir," she said tremulously as he took her hand. "You've heard? Isn't it terrible? How it happened I can't think. He was such a careful driver. Skid. Why, there hadn't been any rain."

"Sit down, Mrs. Jeal," said Collier. "Tell me all about it. He had been down in the country staying with friends?"

"Not with friends, sir. He was staying in Lewes at an hotel, the Falcon. He rang me up from there. I was to let him know at once if Madame Luna called. He told you about that Madame Luna?"

"Yes. Lewes. I see. Did you know he was coming back?"

"No, And that's not like him. He knows I like to air his bed and get everything ready. And it's not like him to drive at night. He was never one for that."

"Unless something unforeseen and urgent—" murmured Collier half to himself. "You must be brave," he added as she began to cry again.

She stood up. "I must go back. I've got to be near if he should want me. Mr. Collier, sir," she laid her work-worn hand on his arm. "He was always one to stand up for the weak. He makes it his business to hunt down wrongdoers. People who do that make enemies. Do you take my meaning?"

"Not altogether."

"Then I'll make it more plain. Mark my words. This was no accident."

She left him to his thoughts. She had scarcely gone when the matron re-appeared.

"I'm glad you haven't gone yet," she said. "I've just seen the nurse who was on duty when your friend was brought in. She tells me she found a scrap of paper with some words in pencil scribbled on it inside one of his shoes. Your name is Collier?"

"Yes. May I see it?" he said eagerly.

She held out a crumpled page torn from a pocket calendar. Collier took it to the window.

There was a prolonged pause. The matron waited without any display of impatience. Collier, looking round at last, observed her with more attention than he had given to her hitherto. A strong-featured, plain, sensible face, steady eyes, a mouth firm but good-humoured. He made up his mind to trust her.

"I'm glad you found this," he began. "It was meant for me. It's a great piece of luck that it should reach me with so little delay."

"Do you understand it? I mean—it seems a jumble of words."

"Not altogether," he confessed, "but enough to go on with. To begin with, a man who's his own master and able to use a telephone or walk out to the nearest post office or pillar box isn't likely to conceal a message, an urgent message, in his shoe. There's something crooked at the back of this, matron."

"Do you mean that his injuries were not the result of an accident? The lorry driver seemed perfectly genuine. The firm he works for is well known. I saw the name on the lorry. Pearson and Galbraith—"

"Good." Collier produced his notebook and wrote down the names. "I'll be seeing him. I daresay he told the truth. He found the car blazing in a ditch and my friend had managed to crawl clear of the wreck. I'm prepared to believe that. It's what happened before that intrigues me. Accidents can be arranged. You remember the Rouse case."

"I see," said the matron. She had lost some of her healthy colour. She was genuinely shocked, but she showed no trace of fear.

"You think he has enemies?"

"He has been investigating the mystery of the disappearance of a woman who came to him for help. He had very little to go upon. I think that since I last saw him he may have got hold of something and at the same time put himself in the power of people who find his interest in their doings inconvenient."

"If you really believe that," she said, "oughtn't you to go to the police?"

He smiled. "A very sensible suggestion, madam. Between ourselves I am an Inspector in the Criminal Investigation Department of Scotland Yard. But I'm not here officially. As it happens I've got a week's holiday starting this morning. Mr. Thor is a personal friend of mine. If I can get evidence enough to put before my superiors I shall lose no time in doing so. The trouble is—the Force is second to none in hunting down a criminal after a crime has been committed—but prevention is another matter.

This message. It isn't clear—but if it means anything, it means that a crime, a terrible crime, is contemplated. Can we—somehow—prevent it? That's the question. We don't know when, or where, or how."

She was silent, watching him as he walked up and down the room. "Thor has ample means. We don't have to consider expense. He must not be left alone for a moment. I mean, if he recovers consciousness unexpectedly—that might happen?"

"It might," she said. "It's not very likely."

"If he does he might say something of vital importance. The nurse must be prepared to listen and to take down every word. You have women here whom you can trust?"

"Yes."

"There's another point. It is my duty to warn you that if my theory is right and there has been an attempt to murder him it may be repeated if the perpetrators discover that they have failed and that he may still speak. You understand? He is still in danger."

"I see. Yes. I must take precautions. What would you suggest?"

"The old housekeeper is trustworthy, but you must not admit any other visitors. Never mind their credentials. No one. If you could bring yourself to tell any enquirers that his condition is hopeless and that he cannot possibly regain consciousness it might be a good thing." He cleared his throat. "I—he will get better, won't he?" he said. "I—I'm very fond of him. He's meant a lot to me."

"I hope so," she said gently. "I daren't say more than that. We shall do everything possible."

"Thank you." He resumed his brisk, official manner. "I've got your telephone number. I'll keep in touch with you. Here is my card. I depend on you. Good-bye. I've got to catch a train." He gripped her hand hard and was gone before she could answer him. She crossed to the window and saw him dash across that quiet tree-shaded suburban road and run round the corner.

"Let me see," she was thinking, "Nurse Stafford, and Nurse Haines for night duty. They're not quite as stupid as the others."

CHAPTER VIII
S.O.S.

THE clock had struck ten some time ago, and John Garland, who was an early riser, was ready for bed. He closed his book, knocked the dottle out of his pipe, and stood up.

"Well, Dennis?"

The young man, who had been trying his father's patience all the evening by his inability to remain in the same place for more than two minutes, was sitting by the open window.

"Wait a bit. There's someone crossing the road. It may be Thor. He's coming here."

They both heard the door bell pealing in the basement.

"Briggs has gone to bed, hasn't he? I'll go."

John Garland smiled to himself as Dennis performed one of his acrobatic descents of the long-suffering stairs. How the boy's spirits had soared up at the sound of the bell. He, too, was relieved that Thor had come at last. He rose to receive him. But Dennis, returning, ushered in a stranger, a younger man than Thor, with a lean, sunburned face.

"Father, this is a friend of Mr. Thor. He says he has brought a message."

"Sit down, won't you—a whisky and soda?"

"Thanks. I will." Collier, without seeming to do so, was taking stock of his two hosts. They went well, he thought, with their solid Victorian background. They were both countrified in the best sense of the word. He liked the spacious, comfortable untidy room with its well-worn chairs and litter of books and papers. The old half-blind spaniel that had been dozing on the hearth-rug came up and nuzzled at his hand.

"That's a compliment," said Dennis. "She doesn't often notice strangers. We've been expecting Mr. Thor all day—or to hear from him. He said he'd come round yesterday after lunching at the Manor."

Collier set down his glass. He had had a long and harassing day with no time for meals, and he had needed a pick-me-up.

"He was staying at the Falcon?" he said.

"Yes. I understood he was remaining a few days longer. I never thought he'd go off like that without a word. I mean— of course I know I'm not much use, but he'd said I might help him." Dennis broke off. "I say—you are in his confidence."

Collier smiled. The boyish candour and the underlying shrewdness were just what he would have expected from this young man. He could imagine how that combination of qualities had appealed to Thor.

His smile faded. "Yes. I know what brought him to Lewes. I don't know what progress he made. He was trying to trace the movements of a woman known as Madame Luna."

"He told us all about that," said Dennis eagerly, "I took him over to the Manor—Belgrave Manor—Mrs. Maulfry, who has taken the place, is looking after Madame Luna's little girl."

Collier held up his hand. "One moment. I want it all from the beginning. Why did Thor come to you?"

Garland intervened. "Is this necessary? Wouldn't to-morrow do?"

Collier turned to him. "I'm sorry, Mr. Garland. This isn't idle curiosity on my part. I must get all the information I can. I can't get it first hand, unfortunately. Thor met with an accident last night as he was driving back to Town. He's in a nursing home at present. He is seriously injured."

John Garland uttered an exclamation. Dennis said nothing but he turned very white.

"The toll of the road," said Garland, "something should be done to check this appalling waste of life."

"You see why I have to know everything he did in the last few days," said Collier, "if I'm to carry on where he left off. By the way," he added, "here is my card."

Garland read it and looked up quickly at their visitor. "You are from Scotland Yard? Then this is a police enquiry?"

"Not yet. Please don't misunderstand me. I am on holiday. Thor is my friend. He talked this matter over with me. He was to call on the Yard if he found any evidence of law breaking. I don't know what he suspected, but he was taking it all very seriously. Unfortunately officials have to rely on material evidence."

"I'll tell you everything," said Dennis eagerly. "He came here the day before yesterday."

He described Thor's coming and how they had gone to Belgrave Down together and met the little girl and her young governess on the hill after their visit to the old church. Encouraged by Collier's evident interest he went into details and was able to repeat his conversation with Quayle at the locked gate of the Manor almost word for word.

When he had done there was a silence. Collier broke it.

"I agree with your father that there's something fishy about that gate. The devil of it is that there's nothing in all this to justify our interference. Nothing illegal, nothing even blameworthy. Of course, we've got to face the fact that Thor did not give either you or me his full confidence. All we have to go upon is this torn scrap of paper found in his shoe by a nurse at the home."

He took the paper from his note case and placed it very carefully on the table.

"You see it is a page torn from a pocket diary, jerked out in such haste that half is missing. That, I may say, is not like Thor. He is very neat and methodical in his ways. The page evidently comes from the end of the diary where there are some left blank for memoranda. On this side there are some words faintly and I think very hurriedly scrawled in pencil."

He turned to Dennis. "What do you make of it?"

Dennis bent over the table. "10A, Fulton Court, W.C. That's the address he gave us. It's on his card."

"Quite. He has a flat in Fulton Court. It's a new block off Vincent Square."

Dennis resumed. "*SO S Collier Garland Lewes*. So is Collier? It doesn't make sense."

"I think that should read S.O.S.," said Collier quietly.

"Oh—I see. *Get the g*—the rest of the line is torn away. Then comes *at any* and another gap, and *first*. I'm afraid it does not convey anything to my mind."

"We'll come back to it," said the C.I.D. man. "It isn't cypher. If I'm right in my guess there was no time for that. Have a look at the other side." He turned the paper over.

"This was written in ink, you see, and at some other time. This is Thor's usual hand. Small and rather cramped but very easy to read. It may have nothing to do with the matter in hand. It sounds to me like a note on one of his other cases."

Dennis read aloud. "*Obvious victim*—and then on the next line *of obsession*. Then a part of a word *iously*. Then, on the next line a large bit torn out and two capital letters and an interrogation mark. *F.O.?* Great Scott!" he turned excitedly to the other. "Don't you see? That means Foreign Office. It's something to do with spies. The secret service."

"It's a possibility," said Collier slowly, "but I don't think so. Still, we'll have to bear it in mind, but, as I said just now the writing on this side may have no reference to this job. We've got to concentrate on the other."

"All right," said Dennis. "*Get the g*—get the gold—get the gun—get the gang—by Jove! it might be that. Get the gang arrested. At any—at any rate. No, that doesn't make sense." He drew a chair up to the table and sat holding his head and poring over the paper. "I can't make head or tail of the rest," he muttered.

"There are a great many words," said his father drily, "beginning with *g*."

"In this case," said Collier, "I'm relying entirely on Thor's judgment. He's worked twice with the police in the three years I have known him and he has carried out numerous enquiries on his own into cases that the police couldn't touch because no law had been broken. I've never known him at fault. That's going too far, perhaps. He's not superhuman. When it's dark he has to feel his way like the rest of us. But there's no doubt he's got a flair. I can no more ignore this S.O.S., Mr. Garland, than the captain of a ship could."

"I see," said Garland. "Dennis feels as you do about Mr. Thor. Well, I'm not standing in his way, if he can be of any use to you. But it's all very vague. You surely don't suspect a woman in Mrs.

Maulfry's position? A rich woman, noted for good works. What possible motive—?"

"I'll just have to make a few enquiries," said Collier vaguely. It was a formula very familiar to his colleagues at the Yard. He replaced his precious scrap of paper in his pocket-book and stood up. "A quarter to twelve. I must not keep you up any longer. I'm much obliged to you both, gentlemen."

"Can't we put you up?" asked Dennis.

Collier shook his head. "I must get back to London and start again from there. Thanks all the same."

He shook hands with them both. Dennis went downstairs with him.

"Look here," he said, "I wrote to Thor and to Miss Kent and posted the letters not long before you arrived. Are you going to Mrs. Maulfry's house in Chelsea? If you should see Miss Kent there—"

Collier understood. "I'm to ask her if she's got your letter? I will. I will."

"And you'll think of me if you need help?" the boy said wistfully. It was plain that he was reluctant to let Collier go. "I mean—about Miss Kent—I don't want her to be mixed up in anything—she's so young."

"I'll do my best," said Collier. "I expect she's all right," he added, but somehow his tone lacked conviction. He knew that he would not feel happy about Celia Kent until he had seen her. There were, as the elder Garland had remarked, many words beginning with g, and one of them was girl.

Get the girl.

It was well for young Dennis Garland's peace of mind, reflected Collier, that he had not thought of that.

Aloud he said, "Don't worry. There may be nothing at all in all this. Good night."

Chapter IX
COLLIER CARRIES ON

Mrs. Maulfry's secretary shook her fountain pen and glanced at the big copper bowl filled with yellow roses on the table by her desk.

She always enjoyed the first few minutes after her arrival. The large rooms, shaded from the sun by the striped awnings over the windows, were so restful. Everything was so easy for the rich, she thought bitterly. And yet they weren't satisfied. That Lady Sabina. She had had everything that life can offer, and yet she was always complaining of being bored.

Miss Cole took a sheet of paper from the case and began to write.

> "Dear Madam,
>
> Mrs. Maulfry desires me to say that she has every sympathy with your cause and will have much pleasure in opening the bazaar if she has no previous engagement on the date. Perhaps you will let her know as soon as possible what day your committee has decided on. Mrs. Maulfry is going for a cruise next month and it is not certain when she will return.
>
> > "Yours faithfully
> > "Jane Cole, Secretary."

She glanced round as the door opened. "What is it, Paston?"

"A man to look at the electric light meters, please, miss."

"Oh—well, you know where they are."

"Very good, miss."

Paston went back to the hall where the man was waiting. Paston was the parlour-maid, and, as it happened, she was a talkative and friendly soul when the butler and the cook were not there to keep her in subjection. "This way, if you please," she said chattily, "and you needn't walk on tiptoe. The mistress is away and most of the servants are having a day off. There's just me and a girl in the kitchen."

"When the cat's away—" said the man humorously.

Paston giggled. He wasn't so old, she thought, and he wouldn't be bad looking if it wasn't for the straggling moustache and the way he stooped. She stood by while he set down his bag and groped, with the aid of a pocket torch, in the cupboard where the meter stood.

"Plenty to do generally, I suppose," said the man. "Lots of visitors and that."

"That's right. There's a lot in and out. Rather Bohemian if you know what I mean. Writers and painters and that mixing with some that are high up in Society. You'd be surprised."

"Bridge, I suppose," said the man indifferently as he searched for a tool in his bag. "I don't hold with all this card playing myself."

"No more do I," Paston agreed. "Give me the Pictures. But it's not all card playing here. Mrs. Maulfry's a great one for music. Plays the piano something lovely, though I like something more cheerful myself. I mean, those thundery pieces give me the creeps late at night. Late hours she keeps, but she doesn't expect the servants to stay up. That's one comfort. After ten they waits on themselves. That's the rule here."

"I've heard of worse ones. I'll have to have a look at all the switches."

Paston, very willing to prolong the interview, led the way from room to room. The electrician, who seemed to be in no great hurry, stared about him appreciatively and listened with flattering interest to Paston's comments on the originals of the framed photographs in her mistress's boudoir.

"That's Lady Sabina Romaine. You'd think she was seventeen, wouldn't you. Thirty-seven would be nearer the mark. Mind you, I don't say she isn't a beauty, though I don't care for that floppy die-away sort myself. That—oh, that's the Professor. No, he's not English, but he's a big noise over here, they say. Digging up old things, and that. They made a lot of fuss over him, giving him degrees and that at Oxford and Cambridge last year, and public dinners and goodness knows what else, but he stayed here in this house."

The electrician was trying to decipher the name scrawled across the photograph. "Lebrun, I've heard of him," he said. "You're right. He's a famous man, as well known on the Continent as Evans or Flinders Petrie, or—" he broke off.

The parlour-maid giggled. "Fancy you knowing him. Highbrow yourself, aren't you?"

"I'm fond of reading," the electrician admitted. They passed to the next room. "No children in the house, are there?"

"We had a little girl here for a week or two not long ago," said Paston. "Not a relation, the child of someone Mrs. Maulfry took an interest in. She had a kid here once before cook says, but not in my time. Mrs. Maulfry engaged a young person to look after her and they didn't give much trouble. Their meals had to be carried up to the top floor, but that wasn't my job. And after a bit Madam sent them into the country to get the good of the air and that."

"They'll be coming back."

"Cook doesn't think so. She says the child before wasn't here for long. It's one of Mrs. Maulfry's charities, see. She couldn't be bothered with a kid here all the time. It's not that sort of house."

The electrician grinned. "That sort of house? D'you mean there are goings on? I thought Mrs. Maulfry was an old lady."

"Hard to say what age she is," said Paston thoughtfully, "and, as to goings on I've never seen or heard any or I wouldn't be here. I'm rather particular, I am. On the other hand the servants' quarters are shut off from the rest of the house. Almost anything might happen and we wouldn't be any the wiser. I've thought that sometimes when I've been lying in bed hearing that music just faintly in the distance like."

"Yes," said the electrician. He glanced back at the baize-covered door that they had just passed through. "It's a basement kitchen, isn't it? No, I needn't go down. I've located the trouble. It's in the meter after all. I've just got to tighten up—"

He groped on his knees in the cupboard under the stairs for two or three minutes and emerged with a flushed face and a cobweb on his nose. "Done it," he announced.

Miss Cole, hearing voices in the hall, had come out of her room. "What was the trouble?" she asked.

The electrician touched his hat. He seemed a very civil man. "We thought it might be a fused wire, miss, but it was only a screw got slack."

"Oh—if you're going down the road you might put these letters in the pillar box."

"Certainly, miss."

He left Paston disappointed, for she had hoped he might suggest that they should go to the Pictures one evening, and walked quickly down the road. The letters were all addressed to charitable organisations and leagues whose object was the amelioration of the human race. Collier smiled rather a wry smile as he posted them. It seemed to him that he had learned only one thing of any importance, and that was that Celia Kent and the child had not been sent back to the house in Swan Walk. That meant that it was going to be difficult if not impossible to trace them, unless—unless they had never left Belgrave Manor at all. Young Garland had only Quayle's word for it that they had left. If they had something to hide they would not want the boy hanging about the place. The house he had just left— well, Mrs. Maulfry was a wealthy woman able to indulge in the fashionable cult of ugliness. Collier, who was middle-class and old-fashioned in his tastes, had received more than one shock as he passed through the rooms. The bronze figure holding the lamp in the boudoir, for instance. The Minotaur, was it? A nasty thing. Damnably clever, of course. The parlour-maid had told him it was the work of one of Madame's friends, a Miss Heriot, who had a studio down by the river. "Always in and out, she is. More like a man to look at, and a plain man at that, with her collar and tie and her big cigars."

He went back to his bed-sitting-room in Denbigh Street. He always called it a bed-sitting-room, to the annoyance of his land-lady who preferred to describe it as a flatlet. He was anxious to get rid of his moustache. The hair tickled and the spirit gum made his upper lip sore. A bath and a change of clothing was indicated. He would get a spot of lunch at the nearest Lyons before calling on Miss Heriot. But first he rang up the nursing home. After an interval he heard the matron's voice. "Who is it, please?"

"Inspector Collier speaking. How is your patient?"

"About the same."

Collier's heart sank. That meant worse, didn't it?

"He has not recovered consciousness?"

"No."

"Has anyone been to enquire or asked to see him?"

"No one. Please excuse me now. I'm very busy."

Collier hung up the receiver and went out to stoke the machine. He seldom had meals when he was on a case. He merely absorbed food when he had a few minutes to spare. He was still young, and so far his constitution had borne the strain. He would have to be careful with this Heriot woman, he thought, as he sat at a marble-topped table chewing his pressed beef and salad. Why hadn't he ordered something else? Oh, hell, what did it matter? A nice way to spend his hard-earned holiday. It was easier to be an electrician than a patron of the arts, and he supposed he could only get into the studio as a would-be purchaser. "And it's not as if I knew what I was driving at," he sighed as he ordered a small coffee. He was beginning to think wistfully of the cases that came his way officially. There was something definite in those to begin with. A brick lying among the scattered jewellery in a broken showcase, the gaping door of a rifled safe, the neat round hole made by a bullet.

People like that Lady Sabina Romaine, pampered and spoiled, sophisticated, over-civilized, harking back to the primitive, the music of the jungle, were amoral almost certainly, but surely they seldom broke anything more serious than a licensing law or a speed limit?

He had found Miss Heriot's address in the London Directory. He came to a door painted crimson at the end of a long paved passage between the high walls of derelict warehouses on the river bank. It was a dank spot even in July, and hardly enlivened by that threatening splash of colour. He was about to knock when the door was opened by a little old woman in rusty black.

She peered up at him short-sightedly.

"Miss Heriot's away in the country."

"I know," he said cheerfully. "She told me I might have a look at her stuff any time I was this way."

"Oh, in that case you'd better step in," said the charwoman readily. "Pull the door to after you when you come out a bit sharp, see, or it won't catch, and mind you put the wet cloths back on them clay models, or I'll catch it. It's part of my job to keep 'em wet, see."

"Right."

He found himself in a large bare studio lit by a skylight. A sound of lapping water under the floor and a penetrating smell of Thames mud indicated that the studio was built on piles jutting out from the river bank. He opened a door at the far end and stepped out on to a balcony fenced with a shabby wooden rail. A crazy flight of steps led down into the water and a small and very dingy boat was moored to one of the piles. Everything was shabby, battered, crumbling to decay, but—he was no artist but he realised that the studio was larger than any that would be found in a more reputable district and that the light was good. There was a camp bed, and a washstand behind a canvas screen in one corner, and he noticed a kettle on a gas ring and some cups and plates on a shelf. A number of unfinished works, swathed in wet linen, stood on a long trestle table. Collier looked at them all and replaced the linen shrouds. They were better covered, he thought. He transferred his attention to a few finished figures in bronze and marble or carved out of a block of wood. "I don't wonder the char trusted me," he thought, "she'd think no one was likely to steal these." There was something warped about them all. Even the exquisite head drooping on the long slender neck like a flower on its stem had a faint and horrible resemblance to a death mask Collier had once seen in Paris of a drowned girl. And there was a little lead figure, either a toad with a human face, or a man with a toad's body that seemed about to spring from its pedestal and made him feel rather sick.

"But I daresay she does sell this muck," he thought. "Shock tactics."

Was there anything here to connect the tenant of the studio with Thor's message? He had no need to look at that torn page from a diary now. He knew it by heart.

*"SO S Collier Garland Lewes Get the g
at any   before   first"*

Was he wasting time here? Were the sands of some fellow creature's life running out while he fumbled helplessly for a clue? Did that paper found in Thor's shoe prove that his accident was no accident but a nearly successful attempt to get rid of someone who suspected and perhaps had come to know too much? Madame Luna had been on her way to Belgrave Manor—and had not been seen again alive. Thor had been lunching there.

Collier told himself that he had done wrong to come back to Town. He should have remained in Sussex. And yet it had seemed necessary to get a little more light on Mrs. Maulfry and her friends. The light obtained was not very revealing.

He was standing, still undecided, staring at the lovely drooping head with the name Sabina carved on its pedestal when he heard voices and the sound of a key being fitted into the lock of the door by which he had entered from the passage. He was conscious of a violent and purely instinctive recoil. Swiftly he opened the door leading to the balcony, stepped outside, and closed it after him.

CHAPTER X
A NARROW SQUEAK

COLLIER had acted on impulse. The moment that he found himself shut out of the studio on the narrow balcony that ran the length of the building he realised that he had made what might prove to be a fatal mistake. The tide was out and the balcony, raised on piles, jutted out over an expanse of soft black mud whose shining surface was marked only by opalescent bubbles here and there. If he jumped the stuff might not come much over his shoes. He might be able to wade through it round the projecting wall of the adjoining warehouse and find a wharf where he could scramble back to dry land. On the other hand it might be deep enough to close over his head, and the idea of sinking through that slime appalled him.

But if Miss Heriot and her friend found him lurking on the balcony they could break him at the Yard. Found on enclosed premises. He could imagine Cardew and Sir James listening to his halting explanation. Unofficial. Unauthorised. They would have to make an example of him. It would be the end. There was, of course, a chance that these people might leave the studio without coming out on the balcony, but a pile of folding deck chairs at one end showed that it was often used. He might climb on to the roof, but not without a considerable amount of noise. There was one possibility. The door opened outwards. If he stood behind it and they left it open and remained at the other end of the balcony he might escape detection. He had scarcely thought of it when that very thing happened. He pressed himself against the wall, hardly daring to breathe as the handle was turned. The door swung back against him. Fortunately for him the person who was coming out appeared not to notice the presence of any obstruction. The boards of the balcony creaked. Somebody struck a match and a blue cloud of smoke drifted by.

"Gosh. I wanted that. Do you mind the smell of the mud? It's better here when the tide's in."

A woman's voice, but deep and harsh. "I'll bet that's Brenda Heriot," thought the listener.

"It's a filthy hole," said another, a soft drawling voice, languidly, "but as a background it suits you, Brenda darling. I'm not trying to be insulting. I mean—you're such an old pirate, a sort of female Blackbeard. I always feel Execution Dock's your spiritual home."

"Thank you, my dear, for the bouquet. I know it's a compliment from you because goody goody people bore you. When are you going to give me another sitting?"

"Good Heavens, Brenda, you're positively inhuman. How can I sit still until all this is over? I'm on tenterhooks. Whenever I stop to think I go all goosey."

"Yes. It doesn't do to think too much."

It was a man's voice this time.

"You wanted a new sensation, Sebastian. Now you've got it."

"My God, yes," he said sombrely.

"You're enjoying it?"

"Am I? Yes, it's a big thrill, and I thought I had exhausted them all. From this nettle—but I didn't bargain for all this trouble beforehand. As we planned it the thing was as safe as it could ever have been. That fatal mistake in the timing, the result of a misprint. Now, with all this mess up it's damned dangerous."

"But you are going on?" said Brenda quickly.

"Of course. We've gone too far to draw back. It's all right really, but I can't help being jumpy. It's the waiting. You women amaze me. You seem to thrive on this ghastly suspense. It gives me acute pleasure too," he added. "And yet there are moments when I'd give a good deal to go back a few weeks in time." There was a queer, unexpected break in the carefully modulated precise voice that startled the unseen hearer almost as much as the two women.

"Oh hell!" said Brenda Heriot roughly, "pull yourself together. You should get Streete to give you a tonic."

"Thanks. I am quite capable of dosing myself."

Brenda laughed. "Of course. I forgot for the moment that you were our herbalist before he joined us. Did you really get every one of the ingredients for the ointment?"

"Yes. I had to go to Jugoslavia for one."

"Not the dead—"

The sentence remained unfinished. Collier, behind the door, fancied that a hand had covered the speaker's mouth.

"Shut up, Brenda. You talk too much and too loud, though we can't be overheard here. That man, steering the barge going down the river, is too far off. He's staring though, and the wind's chilly. Let's go in."

"You two are simply dithering," drawled the soft voice, "you'll spoil it if you get really worried."

"Worried! You're lovely, darling, but you're a nit-wit. He crawled clear of the car and was picked up. It was in the morning papers. There's nothing in the evening editions. He may still talk and we can't stop him. We don't know where he is."

"But he knows nothing. He's not likely to recover, is he? I thought you and Streete—"

"I thought so too," he muttered. "I want a drink."

"Come along then." They went back into the studio.

The man, following his companions, pulled the door to after him. Collier leaned heavily against the wall. His heart was still pounding against his ribs. It had been a very narrow squeak and the danger was not yet over. He could hear the murmur of their voices. They might return to the balcony and next time they might find him.

But his luck held. After a few minutes he heard the other door closed and there was no more talking. Had they all gone or had the tenant of the studio remained behind? He waited another ten minutes before he ventured to open the balcony door an inch at a time and look in. There was nobody in the studio.

Collier did not linger. If one of them turned back and met him going up the passage he would be done.

He did not breathe freely until he was well away. He had spent a gruelling quarter of an hour on the balcony and he felt curiously tired. Not so strange, perhaps. He had missed his night's rest. He was excited by what he had heard, but he was also exceedingly puzzled. Thor had made no mistake, he thought. These people were up to no good. But—what was it? Dope smuggling? Weren't they all three too sophisticated to get a kick out of that? They might be addicts, but there was something else, something to which they looked forward, apparently, with gloating anticipation mingled with positive terror. And Thor—that, at least, was certain—his accident was a put up job. Attempted murder. If they were prepared to take such a risk to stop his mouth there must be something they badly wanted to hide. Collier thought hard as he sat at a marble-topped table and drank tea and ate buttered scones. He decided reluctantly that he could not carry on alone. He must go to the Yard and consult his superiors. Perhaps, he thought ruefully, he should have rung up his Superintendent when he left the nursing home at Croydon instead of going down to Sussex. But—he was not absolutely sure even then, and it would not do him any good at the Yard if he was proved wrong. He would still have preferred to conduct the investigation on his own lines and without any official sanction, but he was driven by an odd sense of urgency.

Superintendent Cardew's reception of him was not calculated to put him at his ease. The burly Superintendent twisted round in his swivel chair to stare at him as he entered.

"Good lord! I thought I'd given you the push for a week? Have you been getting yourself into trouble, young fellow? You look like something the cat brought in."

Collier smiled rather feebly at this witticism. The Superintendent waved him to the chair facing the window that was usually occupied by the more unwilling visitors to that room, shifty-eyed men who answered the questions put to them either too readily or after a significant pause for consideration.

"Now then, my lad. Your holiday started twenty-four hours ago. How is it you're not sailing on the Broads or sun bathing in a Cornish cove, or what not? I'm busy, but I can give you five minutes."

"I shall want more than that, sir."

"The devil you will. Well, the sooner you begin the sooner you'll leave off. Carry on."

Cardew filled his pipe and lit it. Collier, who had thought out what he was going to say, embarked on his narrative. Cardew listened with an impassive face, and, when he had done, smoked on in silence for what seemed a long minute to the younger man.

Cardew grunted. "You took a big risk Collier, on that balcony. If those people had found you there and called your bluff you'd have been for it. What's more, you'd have involved the rest of us. Questions in the House and a Royal Commission. I don't say you haven't had some bright ideas in the past. There was that body in the road case, and the belfry murder. But you do some damn silly things at times."

"I know," said Collier, with becoming meekness, "but I think it was worth it in this case."

"Oh, you do, do you? What proof have you—I don't say proof that would satisfy a jury, but just proof, or shall we say presumption, that any crime had been committed?"

Collier was ready for him. "The message found in Thor's shoe. Isn't it obvious that he was up against it and taking a chance to get his S.O.S. through?"

"I can suggest a more matter of fact explanation," said Cardew. "He tore a page out of his diary to wipe his razor blade on and a part of another page dropped into his shoe. I never put my shoes on until I've finished dressing myself and more than once I've found a collar stud in one of them when I've started putting it on."

"He wouldn't write his own address in his diary."

"He would on the front page. Depend on it that's what happened. Who is this friend of yours anyway? I seem to know the name."

"He helped the police in that queer case two years ago. The Boland's Mammoth Circus crime."

"I remember. He's in with these Spiritualist people. I'm surprised at you, Collier, putting any faith in one of that crowd."

"He told the truth in that case, sir."

"Because it happened to suit his book," growled Cardew.

Collier reddened. "I beg your pardon. If he isn't straight I'm a Dutchman. And he knows a lot. I mean he's studied things that don't come our way. He's a big man in his own line."

"Well, well, I don't blame you for sticking up for your pals. But I hope you haven't been going in for any of this table rapping nonsense."

"I haven't," said Collier, "but I'm not going to crab it. Too many queer things that people have laughed at have turned out to be true."

"All right," said Cardew. "We've no time to argue the case for and against spiritualism anyway. Your friend's had a nasty smash up. Nothing remarkable in that, unfortunately. He's in a nursing home, getting every attention, and there's nothing you can do. If you take my advice, my boy, you'll buzz off to Brighton or Broadstairs and make the most of the six days you've got left."

He glanced at his subordinate and observed that he was wearing his most mulish expression. "What do you suspect? Dope smuggling? Not very likely with people like this Mrs. Maulfry. Why, I saw her name only the other day giving away the prizes at some school or other. She may have a weakness for artists and musicians and cranks. You can take it from me, Collier, they look goofy and they sound goofy, but there's no harm in them as a rule."

"I wish I could agree with you, sir. I'd rather be at Broad-stairs—but I can't let Thor down. I was hoping—"

"Not a hope," said Cardew firmly, "unless you can bring us a bit of evidence."

"I thought that scrap of paper might be enough. It convinced me."

"Look here," argued Cardew. "Suppose I agree that the probabilities are that that message was meant for you, and that Thor hid it in his shoe before he started to drive back to London. He had some bee in his bonnet about this lady and her friends. That's undeniable. You should have tried to talk the poor chap out of it instead of encouraging him and taking it all for gospel. I'm surprised at you, Collier. Don't we get dozens of people with obsessions writing letters to the Commissioner or calling at the Yard to give themselves up for murders they couldn't have committed, or warn us of plots to blow up Cleopatra's Needle or poison the Archbishop of Canterbury. Now hop it. I've promised to meet the wife and take her to the theatre."

He got up, closed his desk, and reached for his hat. On his way out he had to leave a report with the Assistant Commissioner, who had not yet left the building. Sir James Mercer was slightly irritated. He glanced rather pointedly at the clock. The Superintendent felt that an apology or at least an explanation was required of him.

"Sorry I'm a few minutes behind time, Sir James. I've been detained by Inspector Collier."

"I thought you gave him seven days' leave after that Hamburg business."

"So I did. And he took a busman's holiday and got so worked up about some woman who fell over a cliff down in Devonshire that he had to come and tell me all about it."

"Fell over a cliff, eh? When?"

"About ten days ago. It was an accident. Absolutely," said Cardew rather hastily. Mrs. Cardew would be waiting for him at the Corner House. "Was there an inquest?"

"Oh yes. The coroner's jury were unanimous"—the moment he had said it he knew he had made a mistake. Sir James had a vast contempt for coroners' juries and their verdicts. He saw that Mrs. Cardew would have to wait a little longer.

"I'd take Collier's word against any twelve good men and true," said the Assistant Commissioner, "but of course we can't go butting in on the affairs of the county police. If they're satisfied that's that. What did Collier know about it anyhow? He hasn't been down to Devonshire?"

"He got the story from a friend of his, and now the friend's been badly injured in a motor smash and Collier feels he has to take his place."

Sir James frowned. "I like my men to spend their holidays getting fit. I'll have a word with Collier myself."

"I'm sorry, Sir James. I'm afraid he's gone. I told him to drop it. I hope he means to take my advice. A man of his experience falling for a yarn about well-known people belonging to some sort of secret society bumping off people who get in their way—"

Sir James, who had been lighting a cigar, glanced up quickly.

"Good Heavens!" his tone betrayed mingled surprise and amusement, "most exciting. Why has the Yard been left to hear all about it from this young man?"

"There's nothing in it, Sir James," protested Cardew.

"What a pity. But—are you sure?"

Cardew tried not to look at the clock. He answered stolidly. "It all sounded very unlikely to me."

"I daresay," said the Assistant Commissioner rather drily. He knew Cardew to be a reliable man, but he was lacking in imagination, safe but never brilliant.

"The trouble with Collier is that he's almost too keen," complained Cardew.

"*Surtout pas trop de zele,*" murmured Sir James.

"I beg your pardon, sir?"

"Oh, nothing. Who are these well-known people? Did he give any names?"

"He mentioned a Mrs. Maulfry."

Sir James stared, and then laughed. "I've met the lady. I grant she's eccentric, but she can afford to be. She's very charitable, and—you wouldn't know—but she's done a lot for music in England. And she's very well connected. Anyone else?"

"A Mr. Quayle," said Cardew reluctantly. He did not join in when Sir James laughed again. It was characteristic of Cardew that though he had ridiculed Collier's story himself he rather resented the same attitude in anyone else. Collier, after all, was his subordinate and had been, in a sense, his discovery, and his carping manner covered a real respect for those qualities in the younger man that he himself lacked.

"Oh, Quayle," said Sir James. "A censor of morals might find something to say about him, but I imagine he's careful to keep within the law over here. He's abroad quite a lot. He, too, is a personage in his way, Cardew, and a very wealthy man. He gave some priceless Chinese jade to the South Kensington Museum a year or two ago, and he helped to finance the party that is excavating in Guatemala at this moment. And do you mean to say that these are the people Collier has been trailing?"

"Yes." Something prompted Cardew to add, "He nearly got caught this afternoon on enclosed premises, where he hadn't a shadow of a right to be, listening behind a door."

"Good God!" Sir James was quite serious now. "You must stop him, Cardew. These people have a lot of influence. The rights of the citizen, and all the rest of it. Questions in the House."

"That's what I said to him."

"Good. I hope you rubbed it in." Sir James' face changed slightly. He picked up a pen from his writing table and laid it down again. "Mind you," he said more quietly, "Collier's done very well in the past. You mustn't let him get out of hand. I won't keep you now. Good evening."

Cardew hurried off to catch his bus. Sir James, after initialling the last reports brought to him, went down to his waiting car. He was dining at the Savoy with a party. His host was a famous foreign pianist, and it was quite likely that Mrs. Maulfry and Sebastian Quayle would be among his fellow guests.

CHAPTER XI
COLLIER LOSES A TRICK

COLLIER, meanwhile, had caught a bus for Victoria, dashed into the station, crowded at that hour with office workers returning to their homes in the suburbs, and taken a ticket to Croydon. He had tried to enlist the help of his official superiors and failed. He felt he had to see Thor before he decided on his next step. Being worried he was perhaps less on the alert than usual; he somehow found himself hemmed between the edge of the platform and a truck loaded with luggage. Somebody tried to push past him and he lost his balance. The train was just coming in. For one ghastly instant he saw the rails of the permanent way rushing up to meet him. Then, with an effort that seemed to wrench every muscle in his body he jerked himself backward and staggered against the pile of suit-cases. A white-faced girl stood beside him.

"He pushed you," she said indignantly. "I saw him. It was quite deliberate. You might have been killed. I say, do you feel faint or anything? I've got my car here."

"That's very kind of you," he said, "but I'm all right." He retrieved his hat, which had fallen off, and got into the train. Deliberate? Rubbish. It was a pure accident. All the same he had better be careful. He had to exert his will power to keep his hands from trembling as he struck a match to light a much-needed cigarette. Physically he was shaken, but morally the incident had had the opposite effect. Cardew had given him advice that might be construed as an order, and in disregarding it he was risking his whole future. In the bus coming down Victoria Street he had almost decided to hand the case over to a private enquiry agent. No one who knew all the circumstances could blame him for that, Thor himself would never blame him. But he knew now that he could not do it. It was nice of that girl to be so upset by his narrow escape from death. Natural, of course. She was pretty, too. He had not been too flurried to notice that. A platinum blonde. He might have been sitting next to a girl like that in a deck chair on the sands somewhere at that very moment. Oh hell!

He got out at West Croydon. Here, too, the platform was crowded. He was making his way towards the exit when a porter touched his arm. "Just a minute, sir. Will you come this way?"

"What for? Oh, very well."

It occurred to Collier that there might have been witnesses to the incident at Victoria. Perhaps the man who had tried to push him in front of the train had been detained pending enquiries. He was ushered into the station-master's office. There were two railway officials in the room and another man who was probably one of the detectives employed by the Company. There was also a middle-aged woman in black with a large shopping bag. The station-master looked towards her, ignoring Collier's "Good afternoon."

"Is this the man, madam?"

"It's the man the young lady pointed out."

"You are sure?"

"Quite sure."

"Where is the young lady?"

"She had to explain to the friend what come to meet her. The porter told her to come along here," said the middle-aged woman.

"That's right," the porter corroborated. "She ought to be here by now."

Collier looked from one to the other. "Would you kindly tell me why I've been brought here?"

"Wait a bit," advised the man in mufti. He opened the door and glanced up and down the platform. "I don't see her," he said.

"You can't mistake her," cried the woman with the shopping bag. "A pretty girl with fair hair."

"If it's about what happened at Victoria—" began Collier.

"Steady on," advised the detective, "there's no need to admit anything. She hasn't charged you yet."

"Charged me!" gasped Collier. "Am I being accused of something?"

The woman answered. "The young lady says you insulted her."

Collier turned white under his tan as he grasped the nature of the trap into which he had been led. This was as good a way of ruining a man as any other. He looked at the woman. She seemed a decent motherly sort of body of the lower middle class.

"It's not a nice thing to have to talk about," she added, "but she asked me to stand by her. A young girl like that—"

"Just so," said the station-master impatiently, "but where is the young woman? I've no time to waste."

"I haven't insulted anybody," said Collier. "It's either a case of mistaken identity—or it's a frame-up. I've no time to waste either." He turned towards the door but the station detective did not move to let him pass. "There's no need to trouble you further at present, sir," he said to the station-master. "Were you a witness of what passed, madam?"

"Me? No. All I know is that the young lady came up to me, half crying, as I was getting out of the train, and said, 'That man has insulted me. I want him taken up.' So I spoke to this porter, and he said to come here, and she said she must just tell the friend who'd come to meet her to wait. I saw her give up her ticket and run outside."

"Oh, you saw that, did you?" said the station detective. "Well, we'll give her another five minutes. And, if she doesn't turn up I think you'll owe this gentleman an apology."

The woman was beginning to look frightened. "I don't want to get mixed up in any unpleasantness, but I've got daughters of my own."

"You could hardly have acted otherwise," said Collier. "Look here"—he drew the other man aside and lowered his voice—"I'm

Inspector Collier, of Scotland Yard. I believe this is a frame-up, but I'm in a desperate hurry. No time to go into it. You'd better take this woman's name and address, but I think she's genuine enough, and the girl's probably miles away by this time. Here's my warrant card."

The station detective's eyes were popping. "You mean to say—what darned cheek! Did she know who you were?"

"I'm afraid so. Not a bad stunt, and it worked all right, though I don't know what they have to gain by holding me up for twenty minutes."

"They. Is it a gang?"

"I think so. You're satisfied, I suppose? You've got my name."

"That's all right, Inspector. I'll explain to the station-master. He'll be only too pleased. We aren't asking for trouble."

"Send the woman home in a taxi," advised Collier. "She's flustered, poor thing—and—" he grinned—"It's one way of veri-fying her address. Cheerio."

The station detective hastened to open the door for him and turned back to deal with the owner of the shopping bag.

Collier hurried out of the station. Anxiety mingled with his relief. He realised now that they had planned not to ruin but to merely delay him. Why? Some inkling of what might be happening troubled his mind. There were two taxis left on the rank. He got into the first, giving the address of the nursing home.

"What," said the driver, "another?"

"What do you mean?"

"Oh, just a coincidence like. The chap in front of me picked up a fare for the same street and number."

"Was the fare a young woman with yellow hair?"

"That's right."

Collier's heart seemed to miss a beat. "Drive as fast as you can," he said.

The man did his best, but they were held up for a while in the traffic of the main street. It was nine minutes by Collier's watch, but it felt more like as many hours before they stopped at the gate of the nursing home. Collier paid the driver, but told him to wait. He rang the bell and listened. After an interval he heard cautious footsteps approaching and the door was opened a few inches. He caught a glimpse of a large, foolish face framed in starched white linen before the door was hastily closed again. He put his finger on the bell push and kept it there. After a moment the flap of the letter box was lifted and a high pitched voice addressed him.

"If you don't go away I shall ring up the police."

"I want to speak to the matron," said Collier.

There was no answer.

Collier, realising that he was on the verge of losing his temper and doing something he might regret later on, went down the path again to the gate, avoiding the eye of the taxi driver, whose interest in his proceedings was unconcealed. He was profoundly irritated, and anxious too. He had no right to force his way into the house. He knew that well enough. He stood on the kerb looking up and down the quiet tree-shaded road of detached houses standing in their own grounds. A most respectable neighbourhood. He sighed impatiently.

The taxi driver leaned towards him from the driving seat.

"Well?" he enquired hoarsely, "what abaht it?"

Collier's harassed face brightened. A tall, grey-haired woman had just turned the corner and was coming towards them. He recognised the matron. "O.K.," he said. "Go on waiting."

He went to meet her.

"Thank goodness you've come back. They won't let me in."

"Well, you warned us, didn't you? No visitors. You can come in with me now."

"How is he?"

"Better. Soon after you rang up last he seemed to pass out of his stupor into a natural sleep. His pulse was stronger. We are much happier about him."

"Splendid!" said Collier fervently.

He followed her into the rather dark hall smelling of furniture polish and carbolic. A flustered young woman in nurse's uniform emerged from one of the rooms.

"Oh, matron, please, a man came just now, and he kept on ringing, and—" She broke off as she caught sight of Collier and stood staring.

"You were quite right, nurse, to carry out my orders." Something in the matron's tone indicated that this was the dull child of the class, "but I know him so I've brought him in."

"Oh!" The young nurse fingered her lower lip doubtfully. "But his fiancée—Miss Vere—she—she said a man had been following her and that we were to look out for him. That's why when he rang not five minutes after she left I thought—"

The matron was about to speak. Collier checked her with a gesture.

"One moment. This Miss Vere was a young lady with very fair hair, a platinum blonde?"

"Yes," said the nurse. "Oh, she was lovely. Not so very young when you saw her close to, but then he's not very young either. She was very excited and upset, poor thing, and when she said she'd brought a message from the police—"

"What?" said Collier.

"That's—that's what she said, and that she's been followed. 'Don't keep me standing here on the doorstep,' she said, 'it isn't safe.' And after what Matron had said—"

Collier restrained his impatience and spoke quietly. "All right. All right. Don't cry. That won't help. You meant well. You let her in. What happened then?"

The young nurse cast a frightened glance at the matron.

"She—she begged to be allowed to have just a peep at him. 'He's my man,' she said, 'we're to be married soon. I've a right,' she said. So I—I let her. She wasn't in the room a minute, and Nurse Beale, who was with him, will say the same. I waited on the landing. She came out quickly and she thanked me and ran downstairs and out to the taxi."

"I daresay," said Collier grimly, "it was a damn near run thing, as the old Duke would have said. Where was Mrs. Jeal all this time?"

"His housekeeper? She's lying down. She was up all last night."

"Well, it's better to be born lucky than good," said Collier. He turned to the matron, "I'd better see him at once and hear what the other nurse has to say."

He ran up the stairs to the first landing, the matron following more slowly.

"Inspector—"

"Yes?" He waited for her.

"I'm sorry Nurse Potts was so silly, but surely no harm has been done. His future wife has some right—"

"Yes," said Collier bluntly, "if there is such a person. I've never heard of her, and I know Thor pretty well."

He stood aside to allow her to enter the sick room first. Nurse Beale, who had been sitting by the window reading a novel, laid her book down and stood up as she entered. Collier went straight to the bed in which Thor lay. Though his head was bandaged his face was uninjured. But he looked very ill. His eyes were closed and seemed sunken. He was apparently asleep and he breathed heavily. The matron felt his pulse.

"Not so good," she murmured. "Did he wake, Nurse, when that lady came in to see him?"

"No, matron. I was surprised when Nurse Potts let her in and I signed to her to be very quiet, so she tiptoed across to the bed and stood just where that gentleman is standing now."

"What did she do?"

"She whispered 'Darling!' and she laid her hand on his that was lying outside the counterpane and bent over and kissed him very gently, and then she ran out of the room. Nurse Potts came up afterwards and told me she was his fiancée."

"And you fell for the sob stuff just as she had done," said Collier bitterly.

Nurse Beale looked affronted.

"Really," began the matron, "it seems quite—"

But she never finished her sentence.

Collier had gone down on one knee by the bedside. He was staring at the injured man's right hand as it lay relaxed on the white quilt. "Look here"—he pointed to a tiny red spot on the lean brown wrist—"have you been giving the patient an injection?"

"No. Certainly not."

"Someone has," he said grimly. "Someone jabbed a hypodermic in here. Drugged. He's lying in a drugged sleep now."

"But who—why?"

"Who—can't you guess? The why isn't so easy, but I'll find the answer. They'll have got this address from the porter at the flats. If he'd recovered consciousness he might have helped us."

"I'm terribly sorry," said the matron, "if you're right. But even now I can hardly believe—"

"You've got to take my word for it. It might have been worse. I hardly think she would have been armed with anything worse than morphia. Still, he will have to be watched. If they learn that he's likely to recover they may try again with something more lethal. Let no one in but the doctor and the nurse on duty and keep the door locked. I can't explain now but a great deal depends on it. Can I trust you?"

He looked at the two women. They answered in one breath. "You can."

"You've been had once."

"It shan't happen again. You would know her again, wouldn't you, Nurse Beale?"

"Ah!" said Collier, "but it will be someone else next time."

CHAPTER XII
ACCORDING TO PLAN

ALLIE chattered happily, sitting with her governess at the back of the car. Like most children she enjoyed variety and excitement. Mrs. Maulfry had brought her a golliwog and the smiling gentleman who wore one glass in his eye had given her a big box of chocolates tied with pink satin ribbon. She had removed the ribbon and tied it round the golliwog's waist. "Dear Golly," she whispered as she pressed the grotesque object to her breast. "I want to show Golly to Mummie, Miss Kent. Isn't she coming back soon?"

"I hope so, dear," said Celia Kent.

She, too, was enjoying the drive. It was good to get away from that gloomy house and the dank, sunless gardens shut in by high walls, for a while, though it seemed a pity that they should be out just when that nice Mr. Thor was there. But of course, she told herself, Mr. Thor would not have talked to her and Allie much when Mrs. Maulfry and her friends were present. Dennis. . . . A little smile curved her lips as she sat dreaming. When they had all gone back to Town she would go walking over the Downs again with Allie and meet him as they had met before. He liked her. She was almost if not quite sure that he liked her very much. It was not what he said, it was the way he looked at her.

"Isn't this country lovely, Allie? Look at that cornfield!" Manuel turned the car on to a strip of grass by the roadside after a while, and opened the luncheon basket. He set out their lunch on the seat facing them and went to eat his own a little way off. He was very civil, very respectful, very unapproachable. He never unbent even with Allie, and the child was afraid of him. His rather handsome, swarthy face was always rigid and unsmiling. Was it lack of interest? But sometimes Celia had noticed his unfathomable black eyes fixed on the little girl. It was impossible to interpret that brooding gaze but it always made her vaguely uncomfortable. Still she knew that Manuel had been a long time in Mrs. Maulfry's service and that she had every confidence in him.

After their meal he got into the driving seat again and they went on as far as Arundel. It was at his suggestion that Celia took Allie round Swanbourne Lake while he waited outside the park gates for them. Afterwards he drove as far as Chichester.

Celia noticed that he looked at the clock in the dashboard before he turned. She wondered if Mrs. Maulfry had told him to bring them back by a certain hour.

She and Allie were both rather silent on the return journey. The little girl was tired, and Celia was conscious of a growing sense of oppression. She felt her heart sink as Manuel applied the brakes and got out of the car to unlock the Manor gates. It was like coming back to a prison.

"Will you be locking up again when we've passed through?" she asked.

The chauffeur answered stolidly. "Yes, miss."

"Then I think we'll walk the rest of the way."

To her surprise he did not open the car door for her though he must have seen her fumbling with the handle.

"I think Mrs. Maulfry would rather I drove you up to the house, miss."

"Oh, why? What difference can it make."

Manuel's eyes, so like beads of dull jet, met hers for an instant. "If you will pardon my saying so, miss, I know her ways better than you do."

"Oh—all right."

She sat down again, and remained seated until the car stopped again at the front door. They were met on the threshold by Lady Sabina, languid and exquisite as ever, but in a mood of unprecedented friendliness.

"I've been alone all the afternoon. The others are helping Rina to plan a rock garden or something. I've been bored stiff. You must talk to me, Miss Kent. Manuel, bring tea for three into the music room. It's the most civilised spot in this awful house. The others will have theirs later."

"I must just make Allie tidy," said Celia rather shyly.

This was the first time Lady Sabina had acknowledged her existence though they had sometimes met on the stairs in the London house.

"Don't be long. I'll wait for you here."

When the young governess returned, leading her small pupil by the hand, she found Lady Sabina standing in the centre of the hall, her lovely head thrown back as she stared up at the dusty glass lanthorn in the roof three stories above.

"This place intrigues me," she announced. "The man who designed it must have been fearfully attractive. I adore those tortuous minds."

"It's like a sort of temple, isn't it," ventured Celia. "I mean, all these pillars round."

Allie was tugging at her hand. "Look, there's a carpet. There used not to be a carpet."

Celia, looking down, saw that they were standing on a very dingy and faded square. "So there is," she said, "how funny. I should think it came from one of the servants' bedrooms. It doesn't look right here. I wonder—" She broke off, suddenly realising that she was saying too much.

Lady Sabina was smiling, but it was a smile that did not reach her cold blue eyes.

"How terribly observant you both are. I should never have noticed that. I suppose it was Manuel's idea. Here he comes with the tea."

She led the way into a room Celia had not entered before. The old-fashioned shabby furniture of the other rooms on the ground floor had been left untouched.

"There wasn't anything in here when Rina took the house," said Lady Sabina. "She had it fitted to suit a certain mood. How does it strike you, Miss Kent? You're so delightfully young and unsophisticated, as Mr. Quayle is always pointing out. It would be amusing to get your reactions." There were deep divans, covered with some dark red material and heaped with cushions covered with dark red silk, all round the walls. At the far end of the room there was a grand piano. In the centre of the room, on a pedestal, was what seemed at the first glance to be a shapeless lump of black marble.

Celia glanced instinctively towards the three french windows giving on the small unkempt lawn shut in by the high walls of box and laurel and was surprised to see that they were all open. She made the first remark that came into her head.

"It's funny," she said, "that it should seem so airless."

Lady Sabina was pouring out the tea. "You're fond of the word funny," she said.

Celia flushed. "Am I?"

"You haven't told me what you think of the room?" Lady Sabina persisted.

"I—I don't like it much," Celia confessed. "I mean—the colour."

"But she had to keep to the colour scheme of the rest of the house," said Lady Sabina. "The pillars in the hall, the curtains—I know some of them are so faded that one can hardly tell what colour they were once. Does dark red affect you unpleasantly?"

"I think perhaps it does," said Celia slowly. "Yes, it gives me a heavy, shut in feeling." She pushed her hair back from her forehead. Lady Sabina, who was watching her closely, saw that her eyes were wide with fear. She leaned forward solicitously.

"Don't you feel very well? You don't look very fit. Go and lie down for a bit. Allie will be all right with me, won't you, darling?"

Allie's lower lip quivered ominously. "I want to stay with Miss Kent," she said.

"We'll both take her to her room, shall we?"

Lady Sabina helped Celia to stand up. "Lean on me," she said kindly. "Do you feel dizzy?"

"Yes."

"Open the door, Allie. Oh, here's Manuel. Miss Kent is feeling faint. Hold her up on the other side."

"I shall be all right in a minute," gasped Celia. But everything was turning black. She felt herself falling and held up by what she imagined was an iron bar and was actually the chauffeur's arm. She heard very far off a man's voice saying, "Leave it to me. I can carry her"—and the terrified sobbing of a child. Then—silence.

She was sinking, sinking through the darkness and the silence for thousands of miles. The darkness was veined with red that seared her eyes: it was filled with the clanging of metal and the thunder of galloping hooves. There were chariots vast and formless as thunderclouds and drawn by maddened horses rushing by her down a steep slope into the abyss: she felt the hot wind of their passage and heard the howling of the charioteers. If she fell she would fall under those wheels, and the narrow ledge on which she stood was crumbling. She tried to scream, but her jaws were clamped together with a metal vice.

"Wake up!" said a voice, another voice, and this time so near that it sounded incredibly loud. "Wake up."

Celia opened her eyes and saw Mrs. Maulfry standing by her bedside.

"Oh," she said confusedly, "have I overslept myself? I'm so sorry. What time is it?"

Mrs. Maulfry smiled. "Past eleven. You were sleeping so soundly that I would not have you disturbed. Are you feeling better this morning?"

"Better? Oh, I remember. We were having tea in the music room with Lady Sabina, and I—did I faint?"

"You certainly did. We were quite worried about you. However I thought the best thing would be to put you to bed. Manuel told me you walked round Swanbourne lake and that you weren't wearing a hat. It was probably a touch of the sun. Would you like to stay in bed to-day?"

"Oh no, thanks. I'll get up now. I'm all right."

"No headache?"

Celia winced involuntarily as she tried to sit up and felt something like the stab of a knife between her eyes.

"Well, it does a little."

"I thought so," said Mrs. Maulfry. "Lie down again. I will bring you a cup of tea. In the evening, when it is cooler, I will take you back to Town with me."

"You are very kind," said Celia gratefully, "but Allie—I'm afraid she'll be a bother to you."

Mrs. Maulfry patted her hand, "You are a good girl," she said, "so conscientious. It's rare nowadays. We had a good deal of trouble with Allie yesterday evening. She wanted you. She was inconsolable. It really was a great relief to me when her mother turned up this morning. It was not altogether unexpected, but I had not said a word about it because I was not sure."

"Allie's mother?" stammered Celia. "I thought—"

"She has been very ill," explained Mrs. Maulfry, "but she is much better now, and, very naturally, she wants her little girl back. I told you that might happen, didn't I? But that does not mean that you need leave me, my dear. At any rate, not at once. You can be useful to me in many ways. In fact I thought I would let Miss Cole have her holiday now. You can take her place as my secretary for a week or two, and then we shall see. Now you must try to go to sleep again."

"I don't want to dream."

"You have had dreams?" The something perfunctory in the older woman's tone vanished and she showed real interest.

"What did you dream of?"

Celia shuddered. "Horrid dreams. I can't remember much. Chariots like black clouds racing across the moon."

"Chariots? Dear me. And a great wind?"

"Yes. How did you guess?"

Mrs. Maulfry's smile might almost have been described as a grin. "You said the clouds were racing. That suggests a gale."

Her big bony hands were replacing the disordered bedclothes.

"There. Now you'll be more comfortable."

She left the room, closing the door after her. Celia struggled for a while against her drowsiness, but without success. She was asleep when Dennis came to the gate, saw Sebastian Quayle, and went away disappointed. For a few minutes, if she had but known it, he was within a hundred yards of her.

Quayle left directly Dennis had gone. He was driving himself back to Town. He had arranged to meet Brenda Heriot and Lady Sabina at Brenda's studio. Only Mrs. Maulfry and the chauffeur remained at the Manor. Rina Maulfry spent her time smoking cigarettes and wandering restlessly from room to room. Manuel smoked too, incessantly, but he sat still on the old stone mounting block by the front door. His Indian blood made it easier for him to wait. He spoke once, when she had paused for a moment beside him.

"You are taking her back to-night?"

"Yes."

"It is a mistake."

"Nonsense. She suspects nothing."

"Perhaps not. But she is not a fool. It would be safer to leave her here."

She glanced quickly at his wooden face. "You mean?"

"It would be safer to leave her here," he repeated.

She glanced across the wilderness of weeds that had been a lawn at the dense enclosing walls of Laurel.

"No. You forget I have not bought this place. I am only the tenant. It would not be safe at all."

He said nothing. She turned back into the house. There was something strangely suggestive of a bat about the swift darting motions of the angular black clad figure flitting in and out among the crimson pillars of the hall. It was dark in there under the gallery at any time.

CHAPTER XIII
"PRAY SILENCE"

CELIA slept all day. She dozed in the car going up to Town. Mrs. Maulfry had helped her to dress and to pack her few belongings.

"I don't know what you must think of me," the girl said, "I can't keep my eyes open."

Not many employers, she felt, would have been so patient. Mrs. Maulfry really was extraordinarily kind. Twice on their way up she made a violent effort to rouse herself and each time she opened her eyes the lean, swarthy, hawk-like face was smiling and one of the large be-ringed hands was laid reassuringly on hers.

"It's all right, my dear."

She felt better when they reached the house in Swan Walk, but Mrs. Maulfry sent her straight to bed.

"Paston shall bring you up a cup of hot milk. You'll be quite yourself in the morning. Ah, there you are, Miss Cole."

The red-haired secretary had been in the hall to receive them.

"Lady Sabina rang up half an hour ago to know if you had arrived. I told her I expected you any time. I think she is coming round. I have dealt with the letters that came since you went down to Sussex. I told everyone you were going on a cruise and might be away some time."

Mrs. Maulfry sat down and drew off her gloves. "Quite right. And you can take your holiday while I am away, as usual."

"Thank you, Mrs. Maulfry." The secretary stood demurely, her sleek red head a little bent, a step or two behind her employer's chair.

"You have left the little girl in the country?" Mrs. Maulfry had been smoothing out the wrinkles in her long suede gloves. The movement of her fingers ceased for a moment.

"No. She has gone back to her mother."

"Then Miss Kent will be leaving us?"

"Naturally. But I should not think of turning her adrift at a few hours' notice. The poor girl has no home to go to. I told her she could take your place while you are on your holiday. Of course she could never really do that, my dear Emily. You are a paragon. But I daresay she will be useful."

"You will take her with you on the cruise?"

"Yes. You can begin your holiday to-morrow."

"I am not to come round in the morning?"

"No. I will write you a cheque for your month's salary now, with a little bonus," said the smiling lady. "You are a good girl and work very hard. I am very pleased with you."

The rolling eyeballs, the big strong white teeth, the diamonds, all glittered together as she signed her name on the cheque with a flourish.

Emily Cole, craning to read the amount over her employer's shoulder, saw that it fell far short of her hopes.

"Mean beast," she thought contemptuously.

Mrs. Maulfry tore the cheque out of her book and held it out to her, but she made no movement to take it.

"Thanks awfully, Mrs. Maulfry, but haven't you left out a nought?"

"A nought?" said Mrs. Maulfry gently.

"Yes. You didn't really mean fifteen pounds, did you?"

"You want a hundred and fifty?"

The secretary's light lashes flickered. She had often thought of doing this but she had always lacked the courage. There was something formidable about Mrs. Maulfry in spite of her invariable kindness. But it was too late to wish the words unsaid. She was committed to her course, and, after all, she told herself, the other would not miss the money, and she needed it so badly.

Mrs. Maulfry laid the cheque down on her writing table and lit a cigarette.

"You have something to sell?" she said softly. Emily Cole moistened her lips. "Yes."

"Dear me. Very interesting, very amusing. Very well, Miss Cole. I confess I am curious. I'll buy—"

She tore up the cheque and wrote out another. "There you are. Now what is it?"

"You won't stop it before I can cash it, or anything like that?"

"You can cash it any time to-morrow. Will that suit you?"

"Thank you. Yes." She placed it in her bag.

"Well?" said Mrs. Maulfry gaily, "do I get my money's worth?"

The secretary glanced at the smiling face and blinked a little nervously as if she found something rather daunting in her employer's high spirits under the circumstances.

"A man came this morning about the electric light. He seemed to think one of the wires had fused. I didn't see him. I was busy with the letters. But Paston took him all over the house. In the end he found that only some minor adjustment was necessary, or so she told me. But after he was gone I thought it over and felt rather suspicious, so I rang up the head office and they said that so far as they knew there had been nothing wrong and they had not sent one of their men round."

Mrs. Maulfry was leaning back in her chair, with her black eyes half closed, smoking placidly. "Did you inform the police?" she asked.

"No"

"Why not?"

"I thought you would probably rather I didn't."

"You were quite right. I should hate to have policemen in large muddy boots trampling over my lovely rugs and touching my things with their clumsy fingers. The police were intended to keep the lower classes in order. Was anything missing?"

"I don't think so. I went round the rooms."

"Then I shall regard the incident as closed. I am afraid you put rather a fancy price on your information, Miss Cole."

"Well—I hope so," said Miss Cole.

She had regained her composure. Mrs. Maulfry, she thought, was taking it very well.

"What do you mean—you hope so?"

"I meant—for your sake. Good night, Mrs Maulfry. You'll let me know when you want me back after your cruise, won't you?"

"Certainly. Do you mind letting yourself out? I think the maids have gone to bed."

Mrs. Maulfry waited until she heard the front door shut before she rang the bell. The butler answered it.

"I want Manuel. At once. You can go to bed."

"Very good, madam."

Half an hour later she was opening the door herself for Sebastian Quayle, Brenda, and Lady Sabina. She had heard them drive up in a taxi and hurried to admit them.

"Why have you come at this hour? Hasn't the day been long enough?" she asked impatiently. "And what's wrong with Sabina? Come into the library."

She turned on them savagely when they had followed her in. Quayle and Brenda Heriot were holding the younger woman up. She hung as flaccid as a Carnival doll between them, her golden head lolling on Brenda's shoulder.

"What's the matter?"

They laid her on the sofa before they answered. Then Quayle shrugged his shoulders. "Drunk. She's been on her own since we all met at Brenda's studio about four o'clock. I advised her to go back to her flat and rest, but I suppose she couldn't stick it. When Brenda and I went round there an hour ago her maid told us she had not been in long. She seemed very tired and very excited and she insisted on changing into an evening frock. She had a cocktail to buck her up and then another, and so on. The maid said she was very keen to see you. We couldn't get any sense out of her. She started making a row when we tried to persuade her to go to bed so we brought her along. If you'll put up with her, Rina, she'll be all right in the morning."

"The little fool!" said Mrs. Maulfry fiercely. "Haven't I told her? The approach has to be made with prayer and fasting, with every sense under control until the moment—" Her eyes, as she looked down at the crumpled inert figure were merciless.

"She'll be all right to-morrow," urged Brenda. "I'll take her home with me presently. I've no servants to gossip and tell tales. You must not be too hard on her, Rina. The suspense has strained her nerves to breaking point. Try to remember how you felt the first time."

"All right. She can spend the night in my dressing-room. It won't be the first time. Since you are both here we may as well talk things over."

"Nothing wrong, Rina?" said Quayle anxiously.

"Nothing. We've had no trouble with the girl. She'll have got over the effects of the drug by tomorrow morning. I told her she could take Miss Cole's place as my secretary and come with me on the cruise. She's delighted. I shall let her ring up that young man in Lewes in the morning. That ought to settle him. The *Halcyon* is quite ready to sail, I hope, Sebastian."

"Quite. I confess that if it wasn't for the *Halcyon* I shouldn't be feeling too happy. You were right, Rina. Being frightened is a new sensation and it gives a spice to—to all this. But there are limits. I—I wish I hadn't failed with Thor. He's dangerous. How the hell did he pick up our trail? What brought him to Lewes?"

"He can't prove anything even if he recovers. Only a few hours now. One moment."

She left them. Lady Sabina, asleep on the sofa, was breathing stertorously. Quayle walked about restlessly. Brenda Heriot, standing with her back to the Adam mantelpiece, her large feet well apart, her strong, supple sculptor's hands thrust in the pockets of her old coat, stared hard at Mrs. Maulfry as the tall angular figure in the floating black draperies drifted into the room again.

"I heard you talking to someone in the hall. What is it? You looked pleased. You look like a cat that's just killed the canary."

Mrs. Maulfry smiled. "How clever you are, my dear Brenda. I sent Manuel on an errand, and he's just come back. That's all. That brandy comes from Russia, from the Hermitage. It belonged to the Tsar. Pour a little into the glasses, Sebastian. We will drink a toast before we part to-night. Gentlemen, pray silence."

"To-morrow!"

Brenda Heriot echoed her "To-morrow!" Quayle passed the tip of his tongue over his lips before he drank and set down his glass. The little silver chiming clock on the mantelpiece was striking twelve.

"Not to-morrow," he said huskily. "To-day."

CHAPTER XIV
GOOD HUNTING

SUPERINTENDENT Cardew leant back in his chair to stare at the sergeant standing beside his desk. He looked troubled, and the sergeant could not imagine why, for there was nothing out of the ordinary in the report he had just submitted.

"About this accident," Cardew said heavily just when the silence threatened to become intolerable to his worried subordinate.

"A pedestrian knocked down and fatally injured by a car that failed to stop. We'll have to get the B.B.C. to broadcast an appeal for witnesses, if any, to come forward. These things happen every night almost, but—" he flapped impatiently at the cloud of tobacco smoke with which he was already surrounded not a quarter of an hour after his arrival.

"Look here, Smith. Is Collier a pal of yours?"

The sergeant looked surprised. "Hardly, sir. We're on cordial terms, but we don't meet when we're off duty. He's some years younger and unmarried—"

"Quite. Then you've no idea where he's gone for his leave?"

"I didn't know he was on leave. I passed him on the stairs here yesterday."

"Yes. He came to see me and I told him to buzz off to Brighton or Broadstairs. But now I want him."

"He's got rooms in Denbigh Street. Perhaps his landlady would know," said the sergeant helpfully.

Cardew grunted. "He's probably diving off the end of some pier or other. I wish I was." He glanced wistfully at his desk calendar which recorded the date, the 31st of July. His own holiday was due in September. "Wait here, Sergeant, while I ring up." At the end of five minutes of a conversation that conveyed very little to the sergeant's mind Cardew hung up the receiver.

"Neither Brighton nor Broadstairs," he said with a chuckle, "but it begins with a B, Smith. I'll give you three guesses."

"Bude."

"Wrong."

"Barmouth," said the sergeant.

"Anyone can see you've got a wife and kids complex. This isn't your holiday, it's Collier's. His landlady told me he was out, but had left word where he was to be found. British Museum, reading room of—"

"Well, I'm dashed," said the sergeant.

Cardew rubbed his hands together. "That's Collier. I don't say go and do likewise because if we were all as keen as that young man we'd be cutting ourselves. No. A chap like that is leaven in our lump, but bread can't be all leaven." He drew the telephone towards him. "All right, Sergeant. You can go."

Half an hour later Collier walked into the room. The Superintendent waved him to a chair. "Improving the mind, eh?"

"Yes, sir."

Cardew cleared his throat. "I didn't give you much encouragement yesterday."

"No, sir."

"I couldn't do otherwise, but something has happened since—it may be—it must be only a coincidence, but it's an odd one. A young woman was knocked down by a car in the Lindenhall Gardens last night. The time was between eleven thirty and eleven forty-five. Apparently she had run out to post a letter. In fact her body was found by the postman coming to clear the box at the corner of the square. The constable on that beat arrived a minute later. She was taken to the hospital but she was dead.

Her underlinen was marked E. Cole. She lodged in one of the houses in the Square—"

He broke off. "I wonder if you can guess what's coming, Collier?"

"I think so, sir. I know the name. She was Mrs. Maulfry's secretary."

"Exactly. It's a thing that might happen to anyone, but—"

Collier's lean sunburned face had hardened. "I caught a glimpse of her yesterday when I—when I called at the house. She had red hair. Were the injuries consistent with her having been knocked down by a car?"

"Yes. But they were very extensive. It must have gone right over her."

"Nobody saw the car?"

"No. At least no one has come forward. But we'll broadcast."

"Any blood?"

"There must have been."

"Then there might be marks of the tyres. We may get a line on it that way. On her way to post a letter, was she? That's rather significant. No letter was found?"

"From the position of the body it appeared that she had not reached the pillar box, but she may have been dragged some distance. The letter may have been posted. No letter was found."

Collier was tapping a little tune on the edge of the desk. An irritating habit, but he only indulged in it when he was thinking very hard indeed. "They must have thought she was going to double-cross them. They took a risk, but it might have been a bigger one to let her live."

"If we can trace the car—" began the superintendent.

"Yes. But we shan't, sir."

"You think it was deliberate, that someone waited for her to come out and then ran her down?"

"Just that. But we'll never be able to prove it even if we trace the car."

"It's not like you to be so pessimistic, Collier."

"I suppose not. But I'm tired."

He passed his hand over his eyes. "You thought this was a mare's nest, sir. It's worse than that. It's a nightmare's nest."

"We can't rule out coincidence," said Cardew. "Stranger things have happened. After all—a man gets smashed up in his own car near Edenbridge, after lunching with Mrs. Maulfry at her place in Sussex. The following night her secretary, who lives out, is knocked down by a car in a London street. There's nothing in it really."

"If Thor pulls round we'll get them," Collier said, "but something queer happened last night. I was going out to Croydon to see him at the nursing home. I went straight to Victoria from here."

He went on to relate his subsequent adventures. Cardew listened open-mouthed. "A girl. You're sure? A girl had the nerve to try to push you in front of the train, and then complained you'd been molesting her. Suffering snakes!"

"Yes. Golden hair. Very attractive. And, as you say, she had a nerve. But somehow I don't think it was all planned out. It couldn't have been. How could she know where I was going, unless—I've a notion that she was just behind me in the crowd when I took my ticket. They probably know where Thor is now. The porter at the flats was giving the address of the nursing home to anyone who asked for it."

"You say she got in front of you, was taken up to his room and gave him an injection."

"Yes. And that's why I think the whole thing was carried out on the spur of the moment. She had a syringe with her, but charged with nothing more lethal than morphine. Thor had seemed to be coming round and she silenced him, but only temporarily, I hope."

"Would you be able to identify her if you saw her again?"

"Yes. I'll tell you who I think it is. Lady Sabina Romaine."

Cardew half rose from his chair and sat down again. "Oh Lord!" he said. And then, "Don't be a fool, Collier. That's impossible."

"Well, we don't have to do anything about it," said Collier. "About this other girl, the secretary. Have you notified Mrs. Maulfry of the accident?"

"Not yet. The landlady identified the body, and she said Miss Cole told her she'd been given a holiday, and would not be going to work this morning."

Collier nodded. "May I go round and break the sad news? I'd like to see how she takes it."

"Very well," said Cardew, but he spoke with obvious reluctance. "I'll admit that I've got to the point when I daren't leave the thing alone. But you'll have to handle it carefully, Collier. If we go after these people and fail to bring anything home to them you'll be for it and so shall I. What were you doing at the British Museum?"

"Reading," said Collier.

"That's no answer. Was it anything to do with this case?"

"I'd rather not say anything more, Superintendent. If I told you what I suspect you'd think I was batty. And I may be wrong. And I hadn't time to look up all I meant to. May I put a man on to the back files of the newspapers, all of them, local as well as the London ones."

"Yes. You can have Garroway. Tell me what you want."

"Thank you, sir. Nothing at present. If I can only feel that you're here and that help will be sent if I call for it. And—oh yes—I'd like a man to watch the nursing home at Croydon. I've warned the matron but it's a big responsibility for one woman."

"You really think they'll try to get this friend of yours?"

"They'll try again I'm afraid. On the other hand they may argue that after the smash no one will believe him."

"What are they up to, Collier? It must be something very serious if you're right about these two accidents."

"Yes," said Collier. He stood up. "I'll call on the lady now."

"Good hunting," said Cardew. He held out his hand and the younger man gripped it.

"Thank you, sir."

Collier went first in search of Garroway. He attached a good deal of importance to the work he was about to hand over to a subordinate. He would have liked to search the back files of all the newspapers himself, but he had not the time. He wrote down a list of names and dates for his assistant, and hurried off to catch a bus.

Though the death of the secretary had cast another threatening shadow on a case that, to his eyes, was already more than sufficiently dark it had served to convince, or partly convince Cardew. That was something gained and it gave him renewed confidence. If the matter-of-fact Superintendent felt that there was something wrong somewhere he, Collier, need have no further doubts.

The butler answered his ring, rather to Collier's relief, though he did not think the too confiding parlour-maid would recognise him. The butler was large, stately, and blandly authoritative, a butler out of the top drawer. Mrs. Maulfry could pay for the best of everything. But his eyes, after one brief glance, dropped to about the middle button of the visitor's waistcoat.

"I am sorry, sir. Mrs. Maulfry is not at home."

"Have you any idea when she will be back? My business is urgent."

"Mrs. Maulfry has gone out of Town. The date of her return is uncertain."

The butler was preparing to close the door. Collier inserted his foot. "One moment. Has she gone down to her place in Sussex?"

"I couldn't say."

"Will letters be forwarded?"

"Not by me. Any that come here will await her return. Mrs. Maulfry has been ordered a complete rest."

"Are the servants staying on?"

"You must excuse me, sir. I have my work to do."

"Quite." said Collier. "Good morning."

He walked away in the direction of the river. He had seen out of the corner of his eye an elderly roadman with his broom and barrow leaning against the railings of an empty house, munching his elevenses. He stopped to speak to him.

"Hot to-day."

The roadman grunted through a mouthful of bread and cheese. Collier felt in his pockets for loose change and selected half a crown. The roadman's jaws went on champing but his small shrewd eyes were alert.

"I hear the lady at that house up the road has gone away. Did you see her go?"

"She went about ten minutes afore you come."

"In a taxi?"

"Not she. In her own car with the foreign chap what drives it."

"Was she alone?"

"No. There was another woman along with her."

"A girl, was it, with yellow hair?" asked Collier eagerly. He had an account to settle with a platinum blonde. He had not forgotten, he would never forget that moment when the steel rails of the permanent way seemed to be rushing up to meet him. But the roadman could not satisfy him on this point.

"There was another woman and that's all I can say. She was on the other side like, and leaning back."

Collier added a second half crown to the first and walked on briskly. He had two or possibly three more calls to make. It was important to know if Mrs. Maulfry's friends had also left Town.

He felt tolerably certain that her companion in the car had been Lady Sabina Romaine.

He was wrong. Lady Sabina had woke up at about half past three in the morning with an aching head and a parched mouth, and, after switching on the bedside lamp, had recognised that she had been put to bed in a rough and ready fashion, in Rina Maulfry's dressing-room. It was not the first night she had spent in her friend's house, but this time she had no recollection of coming there.

"Must have been lit," she thought vaguely. "I wanted to tell Rina what I'd done—"

It had been marvellous. She had not had such a thrill for years. From the moment she had seen the man hiding behind the door on the balcony of Brenda's studio reflected in the mirror of her flapjack until she ran down the stairs of the nursing home and jumped into the taxi after ramming her hypodermic needle into Thor's wrist, it had been simply marvellous. Luck, the devil's own luck all through, and a series of brilliant improvisations. She had not told Quayle and Brenda what she had seen, but had made them leave her behind in the studio. She had waited, hidden in the lavatory, until they had gone and the man came out. She had not to follow him up the passage. There was another way to the road through the yard of a derelict factory. She had been in time to see him climb to the top of a bus. She had followed in a taxi and had seen him enter Scotland Yard and hung about until he came out again. When she heard him ask for a ticket to Croydon at the booking office she had known he was going to see Thor. She and Brenda had gone straight to his flat when they arrived in London earlier in the day and had been given the address of the nursing-home by the porter. Thor knew too much. Rina and Sebastian both said so. It was lucky she had her needle with her. Not that she was ever without it. One had to have something to buck one up. She was feeling rotten now, absolutely rotten. She reached for the little brocade bag, her evening bag, lying on the floor with her discarded clothing and sat up, groaning as something like a red-hot wire pierced her brain. The mirror slipped out as the bag fell open. She looked into it and saw her haggard face streaked with the remains of yesterday's make-up. Gosh. She looked her real age. She looked more. Horrible. Her hands shook as she hunted feverishly for the magic needle that would give her back the insolent confidence of her youth—for a time—and at a price. But the price did not matter. The price never had mattered to Lady Sabina.

And so it happened that when Rina Maulfry came in to see her a few hours later she found her too deeply sunk in a drugged sleep to be awakened. A hearty shaking, pinches that would leave blue black marks on her arms. It was no use. Mrs. Maulfry stood over her frowningly, biting her lips. She knew nothing of the younger woman's adventures on the previous day and felt nothing but contempt for her condition.

When the culprit opened her eyes some time later it was to see Paston standing by her bed with a laden breakfast tray.

"Hallo, Paston, why are you doing the housemaid's job?"

"There's only me left, my lady, with the butler and Mrs. Evans. And I'm going on my holiday to-morrow."

"Oh, of course." Sabina sat up, yawning and stretching. "Is it late?"

"Past ten, my lady. Oh, my lady, your poor arms—"

"My arms? Yes. They hurt rather." She winced as she looked at the ugly dark stains on the white flesh. "Must have been last night. I can't remember. I don't know how I came here. I was lit. Don't look so shocked, Paston. Hasn't it ever happened to you?"

"No, my lady."

Sabina laughed loudly and stopped to groan. "Oh, my head. It isn't right yet. What have you brought me? I don't want anything but tea and a couple of prunes. Take that toast away. All is lost except my figure. That's my motto. What's this? A note?"

"From the mistress, my lady."

Sabina read the message.

DARLING SABA, You're still dead to the world, and I can't wait for you. You had better ring up Hugh Streete and get him to bring you down. Bring all you will need on the cruise. RINA. Burn this.

"Mrs. Maulfry has gone?"

"Yes, my lady."

"All right. You can run my bath water."

She was on her way to the bathroom ten minutes later when she heard voices below. She leaned over the banisters. The butler's broad back blocked her view but she caught a glimpse of Collier on the doorstep. She drew back quickly. He could not have seen her, but she felt safer when she had reached the bathroom. She remembered now. She must have come to Swan Walk last night to tell Rina and the others about this man. Had she told them or not? She had been all out when she got back to her flat from Croydon. And then—she couldn't be sure what had happened. In any case hunting and being hunted were terribly exciting and worth while, and there was no real danger because she had not done anything. She had pushed him when he came between the edge of the platform and the luggage truck, but he had not fallen over, and, if he had, she could have said it was an accident. She relaxed her muscles luxuriously in the warm scented water and waggled her toes. Her toe nails were stained pink like her finger nails. Ashtoreth, that new woman in Bond Street, wanted her to try green. It would be a change. Anything for a change.

She had done what Rina told her and rung up Hugh Streete. She was ready when he called for her an hour later. They had lunch at a roadside inn under a trellis of leaves that threw flickering shadows on Sabina's golden head and white silk frock. She was looking young again, as fragile and as exquisite as ever, and Streete watched her avidly. He had never even met her in the days of his prosperity. Now that he was ruined, a social outcast, they were often together. They would be together on this cruise in Quayle's yacht. That meant more to him than this mumbo jumbo at which the others hinted. He did not believe what Mrs. Maulfry and the others seemed to take for granted. Hysteria, he thought contemptuously. He had seen enough of that in his practice. For an instant he visualised his consulting room in the house in Wimpole Street. He had been ambitious, had meant to rise to the top of his profession. A knighthood. And he had narrowly escaped penal servitude. Censured by the Coroner.

"Darling," said Lady Sabina, "give me a cigarette, and don't grind your teeth like that."

"Sorry. Why are you wearing a dress with long sleeves? Your arms are so lovely."

"Don't be nosey, sweet. I have my reasons." Then, yielding to her craving for sympathy, she rolled up one sleeve and showed him the black bruises on her forearm. "That's why."

"Who did that?" he demanded hoarsely.

She observed his uncontrolled fury with satisfaction. "Darling, how nice of you to mind. I can't imagine. Really, I haven't an earthly. But I'm not worrying. No bones are broken."

"You take things as they come, don't you, Lady Sabina."

"Don't be so formal. Call me Saba. Yes. It's the only way, I think. Life is like a swamp, isn't it. One can only get on by jumping from one solid patch to the next. If you stop to wonder if it will hold you it's all up."

"What do you know about swamps?"

"We stayed near one last year. On the edge of Exmoor. Hugh, the blue of your shirt exactly matches your eyes."

He leaned towards her across the table. She smiled at him lazily. So many men had looked at her with just that kind of dumb appeal.

"Saba, what exactly is happening to-night?"

Her smiled faded. "Wait and see."

"Saba, it's a rotten business anyway. Won't you chuck it, and come away with me instead? I—I know I've nothing to offer, but—I love you terribly."

"Darling," she said, "don't be silly. There will be time for that on the cruise. This is serious. Surely you must realise that. I couldn't possibly let Rina and the others down."

"It's madness."

"Of course. We should not get a kick out of it if it wasn't. When you've tried everything else and wrung the last drop of sweetness out the ultimate thrill. . . . Come along. We can't sit here all the afternoon."

CHAPTER XV
TRESPASS

The Garlands were at breakfast when the telephone bell rang. Usually when this happened during a meal Dennis expressed his opinion of the interruption in good set terms, but this morning he jumped up without a word and ran out to the landing. "He hasn't shut the door after him," thought John Garland, "he does not mind my overhearing. Thank God for that anyhow."

He helped himself to marmalade and refilled his cup and listened unashamedly to the eager young voice.

"Hallo . . . oh, hallo! is that you, Celia? I've been hoping for a letter . . . what? Oh. . . . Yes, I see. I shouldn't think there would be any difficulty. We'll get in touch with the owner . . . you'll like that? . . . Oh, I suppose so. . . . You'll write? Promise. . . . Of course I hope you'll enjoy yourself. . . . Rather. . . . Good-bye. . . ."

Dennis hung up the receiver and came back to his breakfast. The windows were wide open and a scent of jessamine drifted in from the garden. The water meadows across the line that ran at the foot of the hill were shimmering already in the heat under a cloudless sky.

"It's going to be a fine day," said John Garland conversationally.

Dennis took another piece of toast and looked at it as if he did not know what to do with it. "Father, that was Celia Kent. I must have misunderstood what Mr. Quayle said yesterday, but it's all right. Mrs. Maulfry has taken her up to Town with her. She was telephoning from the house in Swan Walk. The little girl Allie's mother came and fetched her away, and Mrs. Maulfry is keeping Celia as her secretary while the real one has a holiday. She's taking Celia abroad with her at once. Celia seems very bucked about it. She's promised to write—that's one thing."

"Was that all?" enquired his father.

"All? I call that quite a lot. I wish she wasn't going abroad, but it will only be for a few weeks, I suppose."

"And the little girl's mother turned up and took her away. So your friend Thor's theory goes west," said his father, "and the mystery resolves itself into a chapter of unrelated accidents. I must say I'm relieved."

"Well, Celia always did stand up for Mrs. Maulfry. Eccentric but kind-hearted. She went further just now. She said, 'Mrs. Maulfry is being simply marvellous, a sort of fairy godmother.'"

"Was Mrs. Maulfry standing by?"

"She may have been. I rather fancy she was. But Celia is not the girl to say what she doesn't mean. Poor kid, she hasn't had much fun in her life and she's terribly excited and thrilled about this trip. I'm not going to be a mean skunk and grudge her the good time she's going to have."

"Very noble of you," said his father smiling. He got up and filled his pipe from the tobacco jar on the mantelpiece, glancing up as he did so at his wife's picture. If only Mary had lived, he thought again. In this matter of a wife for Dennis he would have had more confidence in her judgment than his own.

"Dennis, you're sure of her? I mean—some girls would find life in a little country town too dull."

"Celia's not that sort," said the young man confidently. "She loves the country."

"Well, neither of you are tied yet. If you are of the same mind when she returns we shall see—by the way, what was that you said to her about getting in touch with the owner?"

"Oh, that," said Dennis ingenuously, "that's what she rang up about really. Mrs. Maulfry asked her to. She wants to know if she can have Belgrave Manor on a longer lease. Wynyard'll be only too glad, of course. Funny what she sees in the place, but I suppose if she takes it for a term of years she'll spend some money on it. If most of the trees and undergrowth round the house were cleared away to let in a little light and air it wouldn't be so bad."

"Well, you'd better write to Wynyard about it this morning," said his father; "hardly worth while to cable. And you might go over to Falmer and see what Harker wants done to that barn of his."

Father and son met again at lunch. The meal was nearly over when Collier arrived. He declined their offers of hospitality. He had had lunch on the train, but he accepted a cigarette from Dennis and sat down rather wearily by the window.

"It's horribly stuffy in Town," he explained, "and I've been on the go all the morning."

"On this case?" asked John Garland.

"On this case."

"We could have saved you some trouble if you had rung us up. My son heard from Miss Kent this morning. The little girl has been fetched away by her mother."

Collier looked at him. "What's that? Do you mind repeating it?"

"The little girl, Miss Kent's pupil, has been fetched away by her mother. It follows that the woman whose body was found at the foot of the cliff in Devon was not Madame Luna, and that Thor was mistaken. I never quite understood what he was driving at, but it all depended on that woman's identity."

Collier was silent for a moment. Then he said "Where did Miss Kent write from?"

"She didn't write. She phoned from Swan Walk."

"You are sure it was Miss Kent?"

"Absolutely. She was in high spirits. Mrs. Maulfry is keeping her on to take her secretary's place while the other girl has a holiday."

"A holiday?" said Collier grimly. "Well, you might call it that. She meant Miss Cole, I suppose. She's got hers all right."

Dennis gave him a quick look. "What do you mean?"

"She was knocked down by a car last night as she was running out to post a letter. No witnesses, and the car went on."

"Badly hurt?"

"Fatally."

"But did they know at Swan Walk?"

"No. She lived out. Her landlady identified the body. The landlady said she was off duty, that her employer was leaving or had left Town."

John Garland drew a long breath. "Are you suggesting that this was no accident either?"

"If we can find the car that ran her down we may be able to prove something," said Collier, "but that will take time, and we haven't too much of that. It looks to me as if we'd got Mrs. Maulfry and her precious friends on the run. Once they're off on this cruise—did Miss Kent say where they were going?"

"No. She said lovely places. Are these people crooks, Inspector? Because, if they are, we've got to prevent her from going with them."

Collier shook his head. "I don't think they're crooks," he said slowly, "not in the sense you mean. But I'll say they're up to no good, and I think Miss Kent's friends will be justified in going the limit to get her away from them."

"You see, Father," said Dennis.

"If she left Swan Walk with Mrs. Maulfry in the Rolls this morning soon after nine," said Collier, "I think it is just possible they have come back to the Manor. I'm going on there now."

"I'll come with you," said Dennis.

"You know the place and I don't," said Collier, "I'll be glad of your help, but it's my duty to warn you that I have no official sanction at present. My Superintendent is sympathetic, but he wants more proof. And if I'm wrong I may get into a nasty mess."

"Dennis," said his father.

"I'm sorry, sir, but I've got to risk it. I've got to look after Celia."

"She may not admit your right, my boy."

"She'll have to. Come along, Collier. I'll take you in my side-car."

He clattered out. Collier lingered for a final word with the older man. "I'm afraid I can't say when we shall be back."

"All right. There's no—no danger, I suppose?"

"I hope not," said Collier, but his tone lacked conviction.

"I see you think there is," said Garland, "and yet you've come down alone. Is that right?"

"It has to be that way," said Collier hurriedly. Dennis was hooting impatiently in the road below.

"Well, good luck to you," said Garland.

Dennis did not speak until they were out of the town. Then he said, "You must not mind my father. He's apt to fuss a bit. But I've made him understand that I'm in earnest about—about Celia Kent. I say, do you think we shall be able to get her away from that crowd?"

Collier was silent for a moment. Then he said, "We can't force her away, you know. You are not related to her, and even if you were I gather that she's of age."

"Yes, just."

"Well, there you are. If she prefers to remain with her present employer we can't prevent it. I'm hoping you will be able to persuade her."

"Is that your only object?"

"No. I want to know definitely where the little girl is. I don't want to be fobbed off with second hand accounts of how her mother came to fetch her away. Frankly, Garland, I still believe that Madame Luna fell—or was thrown—over a cliff ten days ago."

"But—if that's so she couldn't have fetched Allie. And, if she didn't, who did?"

"Exactly," said Collier quietly. "I've asked myself that. I've asked myself if she was fetched at all."

"Good God! I don't understand."

"Leave it at that," said Collier, "we've no proof yet."

Dennis had slowed down as they entered the bye-road that led through the valley by Mitre Gap, but they only met one farm waggon, and the village street was deserted.

"What is Mrs. Maulfry like?" asked Collier.

"Haven't an earthly. I've never seen her. Her friend, Mr. Quayle, did all the business. I gathered from Celia that she's a cross between Queen Elizabeth at her most alarming and the sort of fairy who made a habit of turning up uninvited at Royal christenings. I wonder if we're going to see her now."

"I doubt it," said Collier, "and we've no right to shove in. They've got all the cards, Garland."

"You mean, if they won't let us see Celia we can't make them?"

"We can't make them."

"But you've got some plan," said Dennis.

They were jolting up the lane. Dennis ran his machine on to the grass opposite the Manor gate.

"It's still padlocked," he pointed out as Collier climbed out of the sidecar. "Suppose they aren't here, after all?"

"We've got to suppose the other thing. Will you run this machine farther up the lane? I don't want it to be seen by anybody coming up to the gate. Pity the ground is so dry. There are marks of tyres here, but they may not have been made to-day. Tell me again exactly what happened last time you came."

"Quayle came down the drive and spoke to me through the gate. He said the little girl and her governess had been sent away. He didn't know where. He was very civil but he made me feel it was like my darned cheek to ask."

"Is this gate the only entrance?"

"There's a little door in the wall of the kitchen garden. Celia had the key of that and went in and out that way. It opens on to the hill side. There's no road to it for a car. She was not supposed to leave it unlocked."

"I see. Well, that motor cycle of yours is one of the noisiest I've come across. If there's anyone at home they must have heard us arrive. Perhaps they'll come down the drive as Quayle did. We'll allow them five minutes."

He lit a cigarette and glanced up at the overarching trees.

"Shady lanes are all very well," he remarked, "but this one overdoes it. What's that smell?"

"Rotting leaves, and possibly a dead bird or rabbit in the undergrowth."

"I shouldn't like to be a caretaker here," said Collier.

"There never has been one. We tried to get someone from the village. At least father did years ago, but they can't stick Belgrave Down or the Manor. They're very superstitious really. You'd be surprised if you could get the villagers to talk—which you never could, by the way."

"How do you mean?"

"I mean the things they still believe. Why, when I wanted the roof of the old church mended the other day I had to send two workmen over from Lewes and they weren't keen. One of them fell off the ladder and hurt his wrist and after that they both bolted without finishing the job."

"What was the job exactly?"

"Replacing the stone cross on the finial. But it was no use. It was smashed to smithereens when the ladder slipped."

"That's interesting," said Collier. "The church may be falling to pieces but these walls look solid enough. Are they as high as this everywhere?"

"Quite. Old Wynyard had a piece put on and the spikes a year before he died. It was an expensive business even in those days. He must have been mad. No one was likely to break in. He had nothing of value. A lot of old books and junk."

"And the house has stood empty ever since?"

"Yes."

"And the villagers don't like it?"

"They're afraid," said Dennis. "My cousin Millicent and I got in once when we were kids. We dared each other. There's a big oak tree farther up the lane. The trunk is built into the wall and there's an overhanging bough. It's the only possible place. We did it once together and then I came once alone, just to show her I could. But I hated it both times."

Collier stood, smoking his cigarette and looking through the bars of the gate. "If Quayle or one of the others comes you'll ask to see Miss Kent. If they want to know who I am you can say I'm Inspector Collier. We'll try what bluff will do. But I fancy that if there is anybody here they mean to leave us to stew in our own juice."

"The five minutes is up," Dennis said.

"Yes. Run your machine up now where it won't be seen, and we'll get over by way of your oak tree."

"I don't know," said Dennis doubtfully. "We brought up the rope from our swing years ago."

"I've got a little gadget with me," said Collier. "It's really for use in case of fire. Fine cord and a grappling hook and this locking device. I've had it patented for the inventor. A friend of mine. He did a stretch for burglary, but he's a reformed character." He made a cast and the hook caught in a forked branch. He tested it carefully. "Now I'll go over first, and you follow."

Three minutes later they were standing side by side among the undergrowth.

"Now, which way to the house?"

"Down there. You can see the roof beyond that belt of trees. I say—what happens if we're caught?"

"Don't be morbid," said Collier.

They advanced cautiously, stopping to listen each time a twig cracked underfoot.

"OH," gasped Celia, "how you startled me!"

"I'm sorry," said Dennis. "I've been trying to attract your attention for the last ten minutes." He glanced uneasily from the girl sitting in the wicker garden chair on the terrace to the façade of the house at her back. "Is there anybody here?"

"Not just now. They've gone off in the two cars, taking some stuff to Shoreham where Mr. Quayle's yacht is. We're starting to-morrow. Dennis, I'm awfully glad to see you—but how did you get in?"

"Over the wall."

He was smiling down at her. It was so good to be together again. But there was no answering smile on her upturned face.

"I'm afraid there'd be an awful row about that. They must not find you here," she said hurriedly. "I think you'd better go, please."

"I hoped you'd be glad to see me," he said in a disappointed voice.

She clasped her hands. "Oh, I am," she said fervently. "Only— don't you see—it would put you in such a false position if they found you—and me, too. It would be awful. While I'm with her I've got to conform to her ways, haven't I?"

"I suppose so," he said grudgingly, "the alternative is to come away."

"What's the matter with you, Dennis? I told you this morning when I phoned that I was all right. Mrs. Maulfry is being very kind. I consider myself lucky."

"Yes. But she was standing by while you talked to me, wasn't she?"

"Yes, she was. But that made no difference," said Celia with spirit. "I meant what I said. If it's the gate you're fussing about she has every right to lock it if she chooses."

"I'm not fussing," he began. He realised that they were on the verge of a quarrel. "Look here, I've got a friend with me. Perhaps you'll listen to him."

Celia jumped up as Collier emerged from the shrubberies.

"Mrs. Maulfry will be so angry," she faltered.

Collier, looking at her pale face, found one of his still unuttered questions answered.

"You're afraid of her," he said.

"No. At least—I might be."

"Just so. Well, Miss Kent, I think you have good cause to be afraid. Garland is right. You had better come with us now."

"I'm all right here, thank you. Will you please go? They may be back any moment."

Collier made an effort to restrain his impatience. He had foreseen Celia Kent's probable reaction to what she must regard as an unwarranted intrusion since their first glimpse of her as they made their way through shrubberies had shown her sitting on the terrace placidly reading a novel and apparently in no need of rescue.

"That's just it," he said, "there's no time to explain."

"Do come, Celia," said Dennis, pleadingly.

She shook her head. "I'm sure you mean well," she said, "but I must judge for myself. I'm taking Miss Cole's place as secretary companion while she has her holiday. I couldn't possibly let Mrs. Maulfry down by leaving her like that. And how should I get another post?"

Collier saw that it would be useless to urge her further. There were things he must know, and the time, as she had said, was very short. "Miss Kent, did you see Madame Luna when she fetched her little girl away?"

"No. I wasn't well that day. I stayed in bed. I didn't even see Allie to say good-bye."

"Did she come here or to the house in Swan Walk?"

"Oh—here."

"By car?"

"I don't know. I was asleep."

"Very heavy and drowsy, eh?"

"Yes. How did you know?"

"It was just a guess. Look here, Miss Kent, I want to go through the house."

"You can't do that," she cried. "Dennis, it's impossible."

"Miss Kent, I am Inspector Collier, of the Criminal Investigation Department at New Scotland Yard, and I am trying to trace this woman who is missing, Madame Luna. I advise you for your own sake to leave this place now. Garland, see if you can persuade her while I am going through the house. If she will go take her back to Lewes in your side car and then return here and wait for me."

Without waiting for an answer he stepped through the french window that stood open close to Celia's chair.

Celia looked distressed. "There'll be a ghastly row if Mrs. Maulfry comes back and finds him prowling over the house. I thought even the police couldn't come into houses without a search warrant. He hasn't got one, has he? Is he really a friend of yours?"

"He's a friend of Thor's. I haven't known him long," Dennis confessed, "but he seems a good sort. Celia"—he was holding her arm now—"why won't you come? Don't you understand? I want you to marry me—Suffering snakes! I believe they're coming back."

She was listening. "Yes. They've stopped at the gate. Dennis— you must hide. Behind those bushes. Quick!"

Dennis bit his lip hard. He hated leaving her, but he realised that it would be she who would suffer if he was found with her.

"All right," he said hurriedly, "but I shan't be far away. If—if anything happened that you wanted me badly call out. I shall be within hearing."

"Nonsense, Dennis. I shall be all right if only you'll go—"

He pulled her to him, gave a quick shy peck at her cheek, and plunged back into the laurel bushes.

Celia sat down again, with a scarlet face, and reached mechanically for her book. The two cars were coming up the drive now, Mrs. Maulfry's Rolls, driven by Manuel, and Mr. Quayle's Bentley. That detective must have heard them too, in time to get out by the back door. But would he hear if he was in one of the rooms at the back? She saw that her hands were trembling and tried to steady them. Was it a part of her duty to go and meet her employer? Reluctantly she laid down her book and walked round the house to the entrance. The two cars were drawn up before the door. Mrs. Maulfry and her friends were standing in a little group on the steps. Lady Sabina was lighting a cigarette from a match held by a pallid, sulky-looking youngish man whom Celia had seen the day Thor had come to lunch. Quayle and the queer mannish-looking woman with the harsh voice both turned their heads to look at her as she approached rather uncertainly. Quayle, who was hatless, bowed and beamed at her with his usual effusiveness, but Miss Heriot made no sign of recognition.

Mrs. Maulfry, who was pulling off her long suede gloves, greeted her with careless good humour.

"There you are, Miss Kent. Make some tea, will you? We're all thirsty."

"I'd rather have a cocktail," said Lady Sabina.

"Not to-day, darling. You're on a diet. We all are."

"What difference can it make?"

Celia heard no more. She had gone round the group and was crossing the hall, where already the shadows were gathering behind the red stuccoed pillars that upheld the gallery, on her way to the kitchen. As she went she listened anxiously for any sound on the floor above that would indicate that the detective was still in the house, but the silence was unbroken.

There was an oil stove in the big, old-fashioned kitchen, and three packing cases filled with tins and cartons of provisions had been opened by Manuel. The contents of a fourth that had been standing there previously had been arranged on the dresser shelves. Apparently the case itself had been used for packing stuff to be taken to the yacht. Celia remembered seeing Mr. Quayle and the chauffeur carry it out to the Rolls just before they started for Shoreham.

Mr. Quayle seemed to find it very heavy. His ugly pallid face was shining with sweat and he breathed heavily. Neither of them had noticed Celia coming down the dark passage from her bedroom. She had been sent to lie down directly they arrived from Town. Mr. Quayle had been waiting to receive them. He had looked very hot and bothered, she thought. Apparently he had some bad news to impart and he wanted her out of the way. She wondered what it could be, and hoped it was not anything that would mean abandoning the cruise.

She had lain down half an hour without feeling any inclination to sleep. At last, after another quarter of an hour of wondering how long she was expected to remain in her room, she had got up with some idea of fetching her suit-case from the car. But after seeing Mr. Quayle and the chauffeur handling that heavy packing case she had turned and tiptoed back to her room and lain down again on the bed until Mrs. Maulfry fetched her just before the whole party left in the two cars for Shoreham. There had been something about the two men, silent but for their laboured breathing, that had made a curious impression on her mind. She had been so flurried by the unexpected appearance of Dennis and the detective that she had forgotten all about it, but now she recalled it, and found herself wondering uneasily if there was really something wrong about these people. Smuggling. Could it be smuggling?

But smuggling meant bringing things into the country, not taking them out.

She was standing by the oil stove waiting for the kettle to boil when Manuel came in from the yard. He glanced at the tray she had prepared with cups and milk and sugar and slices of lemon and nodded approval.

"That is good," he said, in his faintly foreign accent. "That is how madame likes it. Will you go to the music room now? Madame has asked for you. I will bring the tea when the water is ready."

"All right. Did you have an accident yesterday, Manuel?"

"No," he said. It was so dark in the kitchen that she could hardly see his face.

Suddenly she felt nervous. "I just wondered," she hurried on, "because I noticed that one of the mud guards was dinted."

He said nothing at all to that. As she left him standing by the stove and went back the way she had come from the servants' quarters to the front of the house she wondered why she had tried to make conversation with Manuel. "It's silly to say more than is absolutely necessary," she told herself. Probably he had hoped that dint on the mudguard would not be noticed.

Mrs. Maulfry was playing when she entered the music room, an angular black-clad figure bolt upright on the music stool, with her loose sleeves flapping like the wings of some huge black bird. She was playing a study by Chopin and the showers of notes pattered like rain on a glass roof, the slow heavy drops that come before a storm.

The others were sprawling on the deep cushioned divans all round the room, silent and motionless, listening.

Celia stood by the piano until Mrs. Maulfry lifted her large, powerful hands from the keys and looked at her with a flash of the big white teeth in the sallow face and a glint of white eyeballs.

"My dear child, a few days from now we shall be sun-bathing, and you have no idea of the heat of the sun in the south. You will be flayed alive if you go unprepared. You must begin now to rub yourself with oil. There is a special oil for the purpose. After tea Lady Sabina will show you how to use it. Ah, here is the tea."

Manuel came in with the tray. Celia, rather shyly, carried round the cups. Quayle smirked at her and called her Hebe. The others took their cups from her without even a word of thanks. Mrs. Maulfry drank her tea quickly and began to play again. It was strange music, Celia thought. She broke off abruptly after only a few bars. "Time is passing. Take her now, Sabina." The beauty stood up at once and looked smilingly at Celia.

"Come into my room," she said softly, "I will show you how to anoint yourself."

Celia looked up doubtfully into those very blue eyes. "I—I— don't know that I want to sunbathe."

"You will have to," said the other, "the sun is everywhere. You cannot get away from him. He is light, he is life."

There was a strange lifting lilt in her voice. Brenda Heriot sprang up and gripped her arm.

"Careful, Sabina. Pull yourself together," she muttered.

Celia was puzzled, and uncomfortable. Was she really expected to undress and rub herself with oil before a complete stranger? When they were outside the room she turned to her companion.

"If you'll give me the oil, Lady Sabina, I'll use it any way you tell me, but I'd rather go to my own room and do it by myself, please."

Lady Sabina, who seemed in an unusually good temper, laughed a little.

"Very well, if you'd rather. Just wait here while I get the stuff."

She came back almost at once with a small round tin box.

"It's not oil exactly. It's more a sort of ointment," she explained. "You must rub it lightly all over your arms and legs and body. Don't hurry over it. Have you got a watch?"

"Yes."

"Then you can time yourself. Go on rubbing it in for twenty minutes." She glanced at the watch on her own wrist. "Five past six. I'll allow you five minutes to get your clothes off and come at half past six to see how you are getting on." Celia hesitated. "Need I do it this evening? I mean—it takes some days to get to the Riviera by sea, doesn't it?"

"Yes, of course. But one's skin must be prepared. I am going to use it too. We all are."

"Oh, I see—" murmured Celia. She was feeling rather dazed. All this rushing about in cars and doing odd and unexpected things gave her a queer, uprooted feeling. But her main sensation at that moment was one of honest admiration for the elder woman's beauty, so fragile and so exquisite. Perhaps Lady Sabina read her thoughts for her lovely face changed slightly.

"What is it? Why do you look at me?"

"Was I staring rudely? I'm sorry. I couldn't help it. You're so wonderful."

Lady Sabina looked at her for a moment very strangely. Then, abruptly, she turned away. Celia, feeling rather snubbed, went into her bedroom and closed the door. She began to undress mechanically, her thoughts elsewhere. All these people were so queer and different to any she had known before, but they were kind to her. It was thoughtful of Mrs. Maulfry to prepare her for the painful results of sun-bathing. Why, even in England it was easy to get blisters on one's neck and arms. They were kind; and she was repaying their kindness by letting Dennis and that detective pry into their affairs. Was Dennis still hiding among the laurels? He had said he would be close at hand if he was wanted. It was absurd, of course, she told herself, but it was very sweet of him. He wasn't clever, like Mr. Quayle, or that Miss Heriot, who did such wonderful sculpture, but he was solid and dependable.

She was naked, ready for the anointing. She caught a glimpse of herself in the glass on the chest of drawers, slim and white as a peeled willow wand, as she struggled with the lid of the tin. She looked rather reluctantly at the thick greenish substance within the box. It had a strong aromatic scent that seemed to gain in power as she obediently rubbed the ointment on. It made her feel just pleasantly drowsy. It induced a passive frame of mind. Time passed. She neither knew nor cared how long while her hands, slippery with the scented oil, moved gently over a body that no longer seemed to be her own.

Time passed. The outlines of the furniture were growing blurred and the walls of the room were receding. She left herself slipping out of her body as she had slipped out of her clothes. She was floating, drifting away. A voice said, "The heart's action" and then after a break—"what are the ingredients?"

Another voice replied. "That's my secret." She was being borne on the wind through the darkness. Over the hills the moon was hidden behind a black bank of clouds. Beneath her the forest stretched away to the dim horizon. Here and there were clearings and a gleam of water, pools or streams reflecting the faint light of the stars.

She was not alone. She had a companion and guide.

"You see what I see," he said.

She heard her own voice answering, "Yes." It sounded very faint and far away. She looked back and downwards and for an instant saw her body, wrapped in a green silk kimono and lying on a divan in the music room. Her heart dropped then, like a stone to the bottom of a well. She clutched at the hand of her guide. A voice said, "She's not quite gone."

The guide repeated, "You see what I see." She answered obediently, "Yes."

They drifted on so near the treetops that she could smell the moist earth and the rotting leaves and hear the rustling of the leaves and the pattering of feet.

Looking down she saw shadows moving swiftly in and out among the trees and silver ripples breaking the smooth surface of the pools. All the secret hidden life of the forest was converging to one point. Everything that had life and motion was being drawn, slowly at first but with gradually increasing speed, towards one fated point in space, one moment in time. The place was fixed, the moment was fixed as the centre of a whirlpool into which she, helpless as a leaf, was being sucked down and down. . . .

"You see what I see," the voice reminded her.

The whirlpool vanished and she was back again drifting on the wind above the trees. This was not the country she knew of pastures and wheat fields. The voice said, "Anderida. We are going back."

It was pleasant floating in space through a night that was so dimly lit by the cloudy moon. Only far, very far away down a long corridor of time someone hammered at a closed door, and the sound, though no more audible than the beating of a pulse, troubled her a little. Someone knocking, someone crying at the closed gates of her drugged brain, warning her to rouse herself, to wake before it was too late. She began to struggle, and instantly the hammering grew louder and more urgent. She felt herself falling and clung instinctively to her guide. The knocking ceased immediately and the vision of the moonlit woods that had grown dim was clear again, so clear that looking down she could see little points of green light through the network of boughs where the shadows raced, keeping pace with them.

"Wolves," said the guide and as if he had given the signal the silence of the night was broken by a baying and wild answering laughter. Celia floated on, but her drowsy indifference was shaken. The night air was growing colder, the forest depths exhaled a stench of decay. Sounds confused and terrible rose out of the darkness. She tried to scream and could not.

CHAPTER XVII
DANGER

ALL THE members of Mrs. Maulfry's house party were gathered in the music room. Mrs. Maulfry was still at the piano, but she had ceased playing and had turned on the music stool to watch as the unconscious figure of Celia Kent was carried in by Manuel, followed by Lady Sabina, and disposed on one of the divans.

"Did you put that kimono on her, Saba?"

"Yes, It's one of mine." Lady Sabina answered sharply. "She's been brought up to be decent, poor kid. I don't half like this, Rina."

"You'll feel better presently," said Mrs. Maulfry. "As to the kimono I am inclined to agree with you. You can go, Manuel. Our other guests will be arriving before long."

The chauffeur left the room. His manner was as wooden, his swarthy face as impassive as ever. The others were all crowding round to look at Celia. Hugh Streete was feeling her pulse. His professional curiosity was aroused.

"What are the ingredients?" he asked curtly. Quayle smirked. "That's my secret. It's the stuff they always used. We all do to-night. It creates the right atmosphere."

"Illusion?"

"Partly perhaps. Not altogether."

Streete was lifting the girl's closed lids. "Are we all to be reduced to this condition?"

"Of course not. In her case the main ingredients were more than doubled."

The young doctor sniffed critically, noting the pungent aromatic odour that had been transferred from the girl's skin to his finger tips.

"I can make a guess," he said drily, "aconite and belladonna."

Quayle smirked again, but made no reply. He was sitting on the divan by Celia and holding her left hand. At intervals he leant over her and whispered in her ear, and Streete saw that her pale lips moved in answer. He stood watching them both curiously.

"What do you say to her?"

The brilliant dark eyes in the ugly toad's face were raised to his. He met that dreamy gaze with a shock of surprise.

"I am painting a picture," Quayle said softly, "in her mind."

Lady Sabina was lighting a cigarette. Her hands shook slightly. "Don't make it too ugly, Sebastian," she said.

"Ugly?" he was genuinely surprised. "Of course not. Don't you know that I am a lover of beauty? It is a picture of a past world, but you, too, will enter it to-night." He signed to her to stand back and she turned away, with a shrug of her shoulders.

Streete joined her where she stood by one of the french windows looking out vaguely into the neglected garden.

"That stuff is definitely dangerous," he remarked.

"Naturally," she said with a touch of impatience. "Everything here to-night is that."

Brenda Heriot came up to them. "Danger," she said. "The spoiled children in life's nursery have tired of and smashed all their toys, Hugh. This is the last they have left."

Streete, who disliked the sculptor's influence over Sabina, ignored her explanation.

"What are we waiting for? Need we hang about here? Let me take you for a run in my car?" he urged. She shook her golden head. "We must stay here. We're only waiting for the dark. You heard what Rina said just now? Others will be arriving."

"Won't the villagers wonder what's up?"

"They will be careful. They will leave their cars and come on foot over the Downs. Nothing is left to chance. Rina and Sebastian have worked it all out with the help of the Master."

He lowered his voice. "Who is the Master?" She answered in the same tone. "I don't know. That's a part of the thrill. Not to know."

"I suppose so," he said doubtfully, "but—" His hot fingers sought hers. "Sabina," he said hoarsely, "must you play this damnable game? Isn't love enough?"

She laughed. "Darling, don't be absurd. Love. I've been swamped in it ever since I was seventeen."

"I see," he said bitterly, "it's nothing to you. I'm nothing—" But even then he could not really believe it. He was a self-centred young man. His promising career and the scandal that had ended it had filled his whole mental horizon. It had meant so much to him when she first noticed him that night in Brenda's studio, picked him out of that queer, hectic, ambiguous crowd. It meant the regaining of his self-esteem. He had come a cropper—but he had been chosen nevertheless by the most beautiful woman of her generation. He would still be pointed out. Not the rising young surgeon but Lady Sabina's lover. It was a part of the fatal flaw in his character that he could dramatize himself like that, and that he had striven to be, at any cost, in the centre of his stage. He winced now at the wound she had dealt to his vanity.

"Sabina!"

"Not now," she said repressively. "Look at Sebastian with that girl."

Streete glanced round. The room was growing dark, but he could see Celia motionless on the divan and Quayle squatting on the floor beside her, his eyes closed, a faint smirk betraying some inward satisfaction, on his fat sallow face.

Streete eyed him angrily. He detested all Sabina's friends at that moment, and all the more because he was too deeply involved with them to escape.

"He looks like a cheap travesty of Buddha," he said.

"Shut up. He might hear you. Sebastian isn't the man to forgive impertinence," she said coldly.

"Oh, all right. Anything you say. But he's rotten to the core, Sabina. I hate to see you with him."

"Rotten," she said lightly, "and what are you?"

"Oh, the B.M.C. hoofed me out, and I don't say they were wrong. I'm a disgrace to the medical profession. Charming of you to remind me of it. And since I've been in with this gang I've sunk deeper. But I was hard up, on the rocks, I was tempted. He's rolling in money. He's had everything. He wallows because he likes it. I—"

"If you say you're more sinned against than sinning I shall scream."

"I wasn't going to," he said sulkily.

She was watching his handsome, downcast face with tolerant amusement.

"Darling, it must be fun to feel as wicked as you do. It's the middle class upbringing, I suppose. I grew up in Riviera hotels, half the year with mother, who was too sweet, and almost as beautiful as I am, but she didn't like me much because I made her look too old; and the other half in Paris with father and his lady friends. I don't know what Sebastian's young days were like. I never asked him."

"Why is he holding that girl's hand?"

"You heard what he said. He's making a picture. He's done it for me twice. He's a great artist in his own medium. It was marvellous—but the coming back was—was rather terrible. That's why I haven't asked him again."

Brenda Heriot had left them. She leaned on the piano smoking a cigar and talking in a subdued voice to Mrs. Maulfry.

"Have you heard again from the Master?"

"Yes. He may be late. We are to go up the hill at midnight and wait."

"With the offering?"

"But he doesn't know what has happened—the substitution. Rina, have you thought of the difference in the weight?"

Rina Maulfry did not answer. She signed to Quayle, who rose and opened the door into the hall. The others had come. They glided in, silent and noiseless, until the room seemed full of crowding shapes.

Hugh Streete remained in the window embrasure. Sabina had slipped away, promising to return. He heard whispering and someone brushed by him. The room had grown very dark. He started involuntarily as the scratch of a match was followed by the lighting of the shaded candles on the piano. Mrs. Maulfry's face was still in shadow but the light fell on her gaunt black figure and on the ringed hands that touched the ivory keys. She was picking out a queer little tune that sent a cold thrill along his nerves, and swaying gently and rhythmically as a cobra sways to the piping of the charmer.

He realised that he, too, was rocking to and fro, he was conscious of his own growing excitement, of the thudding of his heart. The shadows about him were moving, drifting out to the hall. The scent of the aromatic oil was growing stronger. Sabina had come back to him. She was whispering in his ear:

"Be quick. Get ready, and we will dance."

He obeyed.

Presently they were dancing, whirling in a circle through the darkness. The music was maddening. Was Rina still playing or had someone turned on a loud-speaker? But what station would send out those peals that seemed to issue from a mad house, sounds as terrible as the breaking of the wave that engulfed the army of Pharaoh. It rose to an unbearable climax. The silence that followed was like a blow, and the dancers dropped and lay panting like spent animals. The scent of the oil had grown overpowering. Streete saw the red-painted pillars, faintly visible now that a gleam of moonlight shone through the lanthorn in the roof, advance and recede menacingly. For an instant he experienced the sensations of a soldier lying wounded and helpless in the path of a tank. Then, with a triumphant sense of release, he felt himself rising into the air and floating away.

CHAPTER XVIII
COLLIER GETS A LIFT

SUPPER was over at the vicarage. The vicar had eaten cold beef and salad and rice pudding and stewed prunes as they were put before him, and, murmuring something about the Galatians, had shambled back to his study. Millicent had cleared the table, it being the little maid's evening out, and had brought out her sewing machine. She was making a dress from a paper pattern given away in a weekly paper, and was having trouble with the sleeves. She had hardly sat down when the knocking at the front door began.

"Blow!" said Millicent irritably. "I don't get a minute," but she got up at once. Callers at the vicarage were few. She turned up the wick of the hall lamp before she opened the door. Somebody, she supposed, must be ill at one of the cottages and had sent a messenger to fetch her father. But the man standing on the threshold was a stranger, and certainly not a farm labourer, though he looked dusty and dishevelled, and the left sleeve of his grey flannel coat was torn and stained with the blood that oozed from a badly scraped wrist.

Millicent jumped at the natural conclusion. "Has there been a smash?"

He did not answer that. He said: "Can I use your telephone, please?"

"We aren't on the phone," said Millicent, "there isn't such a thing in the village. The nearest for you would be the A.A. box on the main road. Turn to your left towards Lewes when you get out of the valley. It's about three miles from here." She began to close the door, but the stranger inserted his foot.

"One moment. My business is urgent. I want to borrow a car, or get someone to drive me."

"I'm afraid that's no use here. The only person in the village who owns a car is the new tenant of the Manor, and I don't think she's there just now. I'm sorry I can't help you." Millicent's tone was now definitely the one she employed with the hawkers who occasionally found their way into the village, but Collier was not so easily rebuffed.

"You are Mr. Garland's cousin, I think?"

Her face changed. "Do you come from him? Is he hurt?" she asked quickly.

"No. But he's in a tight corner. I can't give you any particulars, Miss Gale. I'm an officer from Scotland Yard. This is my card. I'm telling you this because I realise that you can't be expected to trust a complete stranger, but I want you to keep the fact to yourself."

"I've nobody to talk to here," she said, "and it doesn't interest me particularly. If Dennis has got mixed up with the police that's his affair. Do you mind taking your foot out of the door?"

She had been moved for an instant when she thought Dennis had been injured but now that she was reassured on that point she recalled their quarrel. He had not been near the vicarage since. Very well.

Collier saw that she was not disposed to help him. It was unfortunate, but he had no time to waste in persuasion. He had slipped and fallen heavily when climbing the wall after making his escape from the Manor by the back door while Mrs. Maulfry and her friends were getting out of their cars in front of the house, and his left arm ached rather badly. He had left Garland's motor cycle up the lane for two reasons. He was afraid the noise it would make might attract attention, and it was just possible that its owner might need it later on. But these reasons might not have weighed with him if he had realised that he would be unable to get any kind of car in the village.

And a life might hang on his making the right move now. He should not have attempted to carry on alone. Young Garland, an inexperienced amateur, hardly counted. And yet—in his hurried search of both floors at the Manor he had found nothing that would justify the police in taking any overt step. He could not be sure that Thor's suspicions had been well grounded, even now that, since his visit to the reading room at the British Museum, he knew, with a tolerable degree of accuracy, what those suspicions were.

"All right," he said wearily, "but I'd be awfully glad of a drink of water, and a bit of old linen to bandage this wrist."

Even then she hesitated. "Oh—very well," she said grudgingly.

When she came back with a glass of water and a roll of lint he was sitting on the step with his head on his knees.

It was characteristic of Millicent that this did not soften her.

"You'd better drink the water," she said brusquely.

He looked up at her after a minute and took the glass from her hand and drank.

"Thanks. I feel better."

"Hold out your hand," she said grumpily. It was so exactly the tone of a school teacher about to cane a youthful culprit that Collier could hardly help smiling, but she had brought scissors and safety pins as well as the lint, and her bandaging, though it did not spare his feelings, was efficient.

"And now," he said, "I've got to get along. Have you got a bicycle?"

"Yes."

"You'll have to lend it me, please. I'll leave you a couple of pounds on it if you like. If anything happens to it you shall have a new one. Is that good enough?"

He took two pound notes from his note case and held them out to her. Rather to his surprise she shook her head.

"No. But you'll have to make good any damage."

"I'll do that. I promise you. Where is it?"

She pointed to the side of the house. "In the tool shed. The door is open."

"Thanks. You'll have it back to-morrow, I hope. Good night."

She waited until she heard the drive gate swing back as he passed out and then went back to her dress-making. The lamp was smoking. She adjusted the wick and sat looking rather vacantly at the sleeves that would not fit into the arm holes.

Nothing ever happened in the village. She couldn't say that now. Suppose she went into the study where her father was still preparing his sermon, and said, "A policeman in plain clothes nearly fainted on the doorstep. He wanted to telephone and then he wanted to borrow a car. He's taken my bicycle. He was young and looked frightfully worried. He had hurt his wrist. I wasn't nice to him. I don't know how to be nice to people. Sometimes when it's too late I wish I had been."

Her father would look up at her, his pale eyes shining through his spectacles with a complete lack of comprehension. It would take a long time to explain. Where did he come from? Where did he go to? What had Dennis been doing?

She folded her work impatiently, put away her sewing machine, and went to knock at the study door. The vicar answered as she had known he would.

"What is it, Millie? I'm busy."

Millicent Gale sighed. "It's nothing, Father. I'm going to bed. Good night."

Collier, meanwhile, was pedalling, industriously down the valley in the direction of the main road. From the A.A. box, when he reached it, he would be able to get in touch with the Superintendent. The lamp had gone out, leaving him to bump on blindly over the ruts. The back tyre had punctured and he was riding on the rims. It was very dark.

Once he reached the main road the surface was better, and several cars passed him, but he looked in vain for an A.A. box. Instead he saw a lighted sign swinging from a post by an open gate into a field full of parked cars, and trees hung with coloured fairy lamps and a building with lit windows across the field and at the foot of the long black ridge of the Downs. The lighted sign said Susan's Parlour.

Collier got off the bicycle and left it propped against the gate post. Susan's Parlour would combine a telephone with ceiling rafters and Devonshire teas, and among those parked cars he might find one to serve his turn.

There were supper tables on the lawn and dancing was going on in a converted barn. Waitresses with scarlet lips and blue overalls flitted here and there. He spoke to one of them.

"Can I telephone?"

Heads had been turned as he crossed the lawn where a space was floodlit for dancing. His pallor and his torn sleeve and roughly bandaged wrist made him noticeable, but he did not realise that. He was still a little dazed after his fall, and his mind was less alert than usual.

The waitress showed him the telephone behind an oak partition in the passage that ran through the house, and left him. Afterwards he wondered what had possessed him to ring up the Yard there amid the clatter of cups and plates in the kitchen and the murmur of voices from the front room where late comers who had not been able to secure a table in the garden were at supper. His only excuse was that it was the kind of slip that may be made by a very tired man.

Though it was a trunk call he was not kept waiting long. He gave his name and asked for the Superintendent. After a brief interval he heard Cardew's voice. "Is that you, Collier? Yes, I'm remaining for the present. I'm waiting for Garroway's report. He's coming up to my room now. All quiet on the Croydon front. I rang up the matron an hour ago and she said your friend is about the same. Have you got on to anything?"

"Not yet. But I'm on my way to Shoreham now. Yes, Shoreham. Quayle's yacht is there. They are all going off in her to-morrow, and a lot of stuff was taken on board from the Manor this afternoon."

The superintendent, in his room at the Yard, moved uneasily. "What of it? No harm in that. Is that all?"

"Oh, there's a bit more. Is it O.K.? Thank you, sir."

He hung up the receiver and emerged into the warm and scented darkness of the garden with its glimmering fairy lamps and the blare of jazz from the loud-speaker in the barn. He moved rather uncertainly in the direction of the car park. At the gate a young man coming up behind him brushed against him and apologised.

"I say—sorry and all that. I didn't notice you were bandaged up. Been in a smash, what? Hard luck."

It was just the opening Collier wanted.

"Yes," he said easily, "had to leave the poor old bus on the road. The trouble is I want to get on. I suppose I'll have to ring up a garage to send a car along for me, but that takes time, and I'm in a devil of a hurry."

"Right oh," said the other cheerfully. "I'll run you anywhere you say in reason. I can easily get my bus out. She's close to the gate. Good strategic position, what? I'm always careful about that. Amy—where's that kid—oh, here she is. Amy, meet my friend Mr. what is it. We're going to give him a lift. Hop in, old girl. In with you, my dear chap. Where to?"

"Shoreham. The harbour."

The good Samaritan's car was a sports model, built for speed, long and lean, a greyhound of the road. The girl was wedged between them. She had not uttered a word. The young man was, of course, drunk but not apparently too drunk to drive at a speed that kept Collier gasping.

Once he protested. "Hadn't you better—"

The girl spoke then with a brusque impatience. "It's all right. Don't worry." She had a deep husky voice. "You can drive when you can't stand, can't you, Bunny?"

"Fact," said the young man. "S'matter of fact I'm sober to-night. Got to be."

Collier said no more. Sooner or later, he thought, the young fool will kill himself and anybody who happens to be with him. Meanwhile his reckless driving was saving precious time. He sat back, holding his hat, and trying to think out his next move. They had left Lewes behind them and were following the road that skirted the foot of the Downs, they had turned seaward through the valley of the Adur. The tide was out and the estuary glimmered in the uncertain light of the moon.

"Where do you want to go exactly?"

Collier roused himself. "If you'll set me down by the ferry bridge that will suit me. I'm very much obliged to you."

"Don't mention it," said the owner of the car genially. "It's been a pleasure, hasn't it, Amy, old girl."

He had edged his way round the blind corner near the church and backed with uncanny precision into a corner between a hoarding and a gate leading to one of the yards that lead down to the water.

"This is as near as I can get to the bridge. Good night."

"Thank you," said Collier. "Good night to you."

He got out and turned, and as he turned something crashed, a bright light blazed, and the pavement rushed up to meet him.

He woke with a groan. His head was splitting and he felt stiff and cramped. He tried to move and what had been a dull pain became acute. He groaned again, shut his eyes, and waited. The pain did not cease, but it became more endurable. He began to think. He had come a cropper, a tremendous cropper. He tried to sit up and failed. The effort wrenched the shoulder on which he lay and his damaged wrist. He opened his eyes again and saw something dark over him and the leg of a table within an inch of his face. He was lying then under a table. His hands were tied behind his back, his ankles were bound together. He was in a room lit by a skylight, and the moon was shining in. The moon showed him a patch of polished parquet floor and a white bearskin rug. There was no clock in the room. The silence was complete.

He managed to roll over and take the weight off his damaged shoulder, though there could be no ease while his hands remained bound behind his back. How long had he been in this place? How had he come to it? He lay still and thought. He had telephoned to the Yard openly from that road house, a place which was almost certainly used by Mrs. Maulfry's visitors. They would leave their cars there and walk over the Downs to the Manor and return again unnoticed at dawn. What a dunder-headed fool he had been not to realise that at the time. The owner of the sports car had overheard him and had put himself in his way. And now, a faint creaking of timbers, a lapping of water enlightened him still more. He was on board Quayle's yacht where she lay at her moorings. The ineffable Bunny and his young woman had first laid him out and then half dragged and half carried him on board. A smart bit of work, but probably it was safe enough once they were through the yard gate. They had tied him up and left him. Now, no doubt, they were driving back to tell the others.

He wondered what sort of reception they would get from Mrs. Maulfry. They would have to dispose of him somehow, and quickly. If the Superintendent got worried he might get in touch with the Shoreham people, but by that time the yacht might be well away. A scrap of the burial service for those at sea floated through Collier's mind. Committed to the deep . . . committed. . . . He jolted back into full consciousness. A crime was to be committed, and he lay there helpless.

He reproached himself for not having taken Dennis Garland more fully into his confidence. He had been afraid of losing face if, after all, his suspicions had proved to be unfounded. Too late he saw how unfair it had been to the boy to take him to the Manor and leave him there in ignorance of the danger. True, he had not meant to leave him. A certain course of action had been forced on him, and there had been very little time. It had seemed to him then that he would find that the time spent in searching Quayle's yacht would not be wasted. He knew now that he had been right. The festive owner of the sports car would hardly have taken the trouble to drive him down and make him a prisoner in the yacht's saloon if there had been nothing on board that he might not see. And they had already—he was sure of it now in his own mind—they had already committed one murder, no, two, and attempted a third.

Accidents. Could they fake his death to appear accidental? Probably. Hitherto they had shown considerable ingenuity. But the other affairs had been planned in advance. Bunny, he felt sure, had acted on his own initiative. As usual, one thing led to another. Would he be sent back to finish the job? In that case he might arrive at any moment.

Collier made another effort to sit up and knocked his head against the table leg. There was a tinkling of glass. He tried again and the table overturned. Two glasses crashed with it on the floor. Collier, grimly amused, divined that his captors had felt the need of a pick-me-up before they went back to make their report. But the broken glass might be useful. He could sit up now and he did, though for a minute the pain in his head stopped all thought. But then, after much wriggling and twisting, he contrived to get a bit of the glass between his cramped fingers and to rub it perseveringly up and down against the cord that bound his wrists. It was a long business. Once the glass shattered and another bit had to be found. But at last he could feel the frayed hemp tickling his palm. The last strand broke as he wrenched at it and the loosened coil slipped over his hands. He sat for a minute gently chafing them to bring back the circulation before he started on the cord that bound his ankles. He was getting to his feet, clumsily, for he was very stiff and sore, when he heard a board creak. Someone was coming down the companion to the saloon.

CHAPTER XIX
VETO

SUPERINTENDENT Cardew hung up the receiver and re-lit his cigarette. He was not in the best of tempers. Normally at this hour he would be busy with a watering can in the back garden of his little house at Kew, in his shirt sleeves and a pair of old slippers, while Mrs. Cardew, having cleared away the supper, sat over a game of patience. Mabel was a rare one for patience, but you had to be at the Yard to know the real meaning of the word.

The night was warm and oppressive. On the Embankment there was not a breath of wind to stir the leaves of the planes, and the shadows that danced with such heartless gaiety on windy nights over the huddled sleepers on the seats were motionless. "Feels like a thunderstorm," thought Cardew. "Come in," he said. "Oh, there you are at last, Garroway. Anything to report?"

The sergeant, who was a man of few words, stepped forward and laid some typewritten sheets on the desk before him. They were headed. Extracts from *Mardlescombe and Wincy Gazette* on the 3rd, 9th, and 17th of August.

He read them through.

"Is that all?"

"No, sir. I rang up the principal house and estate agents in Town—without result. Then I tried the nearest large town to this place Mardlescombe. Quinly and Bull told me they had a big house standing in its own grounds outside the village which they let furnished during the summer months. Their tenant last year was a Mrs. Maulfry."

The Superintendent whistled. "Look here, Garroway, did Inspector Collier tell you to look out for this sort of case?"

"Yes, sir. And then to find out if certain people were in the neighbourhood at the time. It's been a job, sir, going through all these local papers. I've had five chaps at it all day. Will that be all, sir?"

"Yes."

Garroway saluted and withdrew. Cardew, left alone, sat with his head in his hands, re-reading the typed copies of press cuttings, now nearly a year old.

A coincidence. It could not be anything else. The thing was impossible. And yet Collier had foretold the juxtaposition of a certain type of case with certain names.

The Superintendent was conscious of a chill. He found himself shivering in spite of the close heat of his room.

If it was true it must be dealt with. Collier had been left to bear the brunt of the enquiry long enough. But, if it was to go on he needed more authority. The Commissioner was in Switzerland, recovering after an operation, and the Assistant Commissioner was in charge.

Five minutes later Sir James Mercer, who was playing bridge at his club with Spenlowe, the nerve specialist, Harley Cuffe, the portrait painter, and a pig breeder from Warwickshire named Smith, was called to the telephone.

He came back after a brief interval, picked up his cards, and, after an awkward pause, during which they had waited for him to declare, laid them down again.

"Sorry. I can't go on. Sorry to let you down. Perhaps you can get somebody to cut in."

"Never mind that," said Spenlowe. "You're worried. What's the trouble? Why not get it off your chest?"

He spoke lightly but there was no answering smile on Sir James' face.

"I've half a mind to," he said. "One of my chaps is on his way here now from the Yard."

"At this hour?" commented Cuffe. "Some worker. Don't you fellows ever get a night's sleep?"

"It's irregular, of course. He was waiting for a report which has just come in. He's inclined to be mysterious and I can't make head or tail of it, but if the people he mentioned are really involved it looks like a nasty mess."

Cuffe, a big man, with the sanguine complexion and twink-ling blue eyes of the laughing cavalier, smacked his lips.

"Let's have it—but not here," he added, as a player at another table turned his head to glare at him. "We can talk in the smok-ing room."

They adjourned and ordered drinks. "But I make no prom-ises," said Mercer. "I'm going to wait for my man, and if he says hush hush, I shall hush hush."

"Yours must be a very interesting job," said the man from Warwickshire.

"I'd swop with you any day," growled Mercer.

The other grinned. "Well, you know where you are with acknowledged pigs."

Sir James was looking towards the door. It is not far from New Scotland Yard to Pall Mall, and he had told Cardew to take a taxi and warned the porter as they passed through the hall that he was expecting a visitor.

Cardew entered and crossed the room to where they sat.

"I wouldn't have butted in like this, Sir James, if it had not been urgent."

"That's all right, Cardew. Now the point is can we discuss this matter in the presence of my friends here?"

The Superintendent hesitated. "It's irregular—"

"Quite. But in view of the names you mentioned they may be able to help us. They are old friends, and they will, of course, be sworn to secrecy."

"See it wet, see it dry," grinned the irrepressible artist.

"Sit down, Cardew. Will you have a drink? No? A cigar?"

"I won't say no to that, Sir James. I can't afford the brand myself. Do you want me to tell it all from the beginning?"

"Well—briefly, just a rough outline. I'll ask any questions that occur to me."

Cardew settled himself in the capacious depths of his chair.

"It started about a fortnight ago with the disappearance of a woman, a palmist known as Madame Luna, who had just come out after a sentence of three weeks in the first division for fortune telling. A man who knew something of her and to whom she had come for assistance got the wind up about her. He had a friend in the C.I.D. and talked to him about it, and this chap, instead of making the most of the seven days' leave he'd just been given, started nosing about unofficially and on his own. He found out a few things and came to me about it. A mare's nest, I thought, and rightly or wrongly I tried to discourage him. And then a thing happened that made me wonder if there wasn't something queer." He drew at his cigar. "I'd like to put it to you, gentlemen. Suppose A asks B to lunch, and on his way home B's car skids and he narrowly escapes being burnt to death, and then, the following night C—A's secretary—is run down and killed by an unidentified car as she crosses the street to post a letter. Add to that the fact that B was trying to find the mother of a child who was in A's charge—I'm sorry—without going into the thing thoroughly I can't give you any idea of the case. I should bore you, and there isn't time."

"You suggest that B and C met with accidents because they knew too much?" said Spenlowe.

"That's the idea. But we've no evidence."

"It sounds pretty thin so far," said the Assistant Commissioner. "Who is this chap who would rather find more work for an already over-worked department than take a holiday?"

"You don't have to ask, sir," said Cardew grimly, "it's Collier."

Sir James laughed as he turned to Spenlow. "He's our *enfant terrible*. He's a bit of an artist in his own line, imaginative, intuitive—all that. We've known him to make some inspired jumps at unexpected conclusions, haven't we, Superintendent? But he's made some gaffes, too. We have to verify his statements. What does he suspect in this case, Cardew. I mean—what's at the back of this woman's disappearance?"

"If we could tell you that, sir, we wouldn't be worrying."

"Well, it seems an original position," said Cuffe. "Usually the police are landed with a crime, blown up safe, a body, or what not, and have to hunt for the criminal. You've got the criminal but are short of a crime. Quite a Gilbertian situation."

"Yes, sir," said Cardew, with rather more than his usual stolidity of manner. He did not much care for Cuffe.

"Can't you make a guess?" asked Sir James, with a touch of impatience. "I won't remind you of it, Cardew, if it proves wide of the mark."

"I'd rather not, sir."

"Better tell them who these people are," said Sir James.

Cardew cleared his throat. "The lady in question is a Mrs. Maulfry—"

Cuffe whistled. "The widow of the South American millionaire? Tinned meat from the Argentine, wasn't it? Why she bought that first folio last year and gave it to the British Museum. She does a lot for crippled children, too."

"Quite right," said Spenlowe. "She's a most generous patroness of a Home I visit. In fact, without her it would have to close down. I've heard she does a lot for music, too. If that's your suspect, Superintendent, you'll have to think again."

Cuffe chuckled. "She's a foreigner, of course, Spanish South American, though I believe old Maulfry was of British origin. The police, my dear Spenlowe, are very insular. That burnt out Southern type wouldn't appeal to them at all. I painted her portrait three years ago, and it was hung on the line."

"By Jove," said Sir James, "I remember it. In black lace, wasn't she, with diamonds. An extraordinary-looking woman. Very striking appearance."

"You see," said Sir James to Cardew, "what my friends think, and they know the lady personally. But go on."

Cardew reddened. He did not care for the turn the conversation had taken. But he went on doggedly. "There's Mr. Sebastian Quayle."

There was a perceptible pause before Cuffe spoke. "Another benefactor of the race, my dear Superintendent. It was Quayle who, after one of the most sensational duels the auction room has ever witnessed, saved the Weland Reynolds for the nation. He has added considerably to our collection of Chinese jade. As a collector and donor he's simply admirable. But I don't mind admitting that if you regard him merely as a human being he's a nasty piece of work."

"Anyone else?" asked Spenlowe.

"Lady Sabina Romaine."

"What? The famous beauty?" cried the man from Warwick-shire. "I used to carry a picture of her about with me when I was young. Haven't heard of her lately. She must be getting on."

"You've said it. I painted her—it must be twelve years ago. Ice blue eyes, that silvery fair hair, and a skin like magnolia petals. Her first husband commissioned the portrait. He was mad about her, and I don't wonder. But she ran away with another man before the paint was dry on the canvas, and I never got my money. At least, not from him. It was bought by a public art gallery. I called it the siren." Cuffe chuckled. "I wasn't so far out. Hot stuff, though she looked like an icicle. But you fellows can't touch her, Jimmie, her father was the Duke of Leam. The present duke is her cousin. She's got no end of relations."

"The Law," said Sir James sententiously, "is no respecter of persons."

"Oh yeah?" said Cuffe. "Well, why don't you go on then and round up the lot? You can hold them for loitering with intent if you don't want to formulate a charge."

"You be damned," said Sir James. "Carry on with that list, superintendent—or have we come to the end of it?"

"There's a lady artist," said Cardew dutifully, "one of those that do statues—"

"Makes faces and busts," murmured Cuffe.

"A Miss Heriot."

"Gosh!" groaned Cuffe. "Anybody here seen her stuff?"

"I have," said Spenlowe. "She had a show in Bond Street. Definitely pathological. It interested me a good deal. Judging by her output she's a border line case."

"There's one other name," said Cardew. "Streete. He used to be a doctor, but he got into a bit of a mess—"

They all looked enquiringly at Spenlowe, who shook his head. "I have nothing to add to that," he said stiffly. "With all due respects to the Superintendent I see no suggestion of any community of interests in this list. Beyond the fact that, they might all be fairly described as decidedly hard boiled. And, if I were you," he added, "I'd take warning from that. You might go a bit beyond your rights with some people and get away with it, but not with any of those. I don't suppose you're yearning for another Commission of Enquiry into the conduct of the police?"

"God forbid," said Sir James piously.

"It's highly improbable, Cardew, that these people have committed or that they contemplate committing any serious breach of the law. Collier means well. I like to see a man keen, but you'd better call him off. And if I were you I'd go straight home from here. Don't lose your night's rest on account of this."

"Yes, Sir James," said the Superintendent, but he did not move, and he still looked worried. "That is all very well," he said heavily, "but I've got a little girl of my own."

This simple statement produced an immediate change in his hearers. Cuffe's smile vanished and Spenlowe leaned forward with unconcealed interest, while the Assistant Commissioner, who had been in the act of rising from his chair to see his subordinate out, sank back again.

"What do you mean by that, Cardew?"

"Well, sir, this Madame Luna was a protégée of Mrs. Maulfry's. She's rich and generous and helps a good many, and it seems that when the palmist got three weeks at Manchester for fortune telling, which was wrongly reported in the papers as three months, Mrs. Maulfry went to her lodgings and took Madame's little girl, a child of five of so, to stay with her, engaged a young lady as nursery governess, and sent the pair of them down to a furnished house she's just taken in Sussex. When the mother came out, much sooner than she was expected, she went down to Sussex. She's been traced as far as Lewes, and no farther, unless it was her body that was found at the foot of a cliff in Devonshire three days later. That was ten days ago, but the day before yesterday, according to Mrs. Maulfry, Madame Luna turned up and took her child away."

"Have you verified that?" asked Sir James.

"Not yet. Collier's trying to."

"I still don't see"—said Cuffe—"is there any suggestion that Mrs. Maulfry ill-treated the child?"

"None whatever."

Sir James sighed. He knew that the Superintendent could not be hurried. "Then what is the trouble, Cardew?"

"It's this, sir—" They all watched the Superintendent's strong square-tipped fingers as they drew a newspaper cutting from his letter case and smoothed it out on his knee. "Before Collier went off this morning he put somebody on to looking through the back files of the provincial papers. He told them the probable date and what they were to look out for. Shall I read it out? It's quite a short paragraph?"

"By all means."

"There are three cuttings here, sir, from three consecutive issues of a weekly paper, the *Mardlescombe and Wincy Gazette*. The last sums up the whole matter." He cleared his throat again.

"The search for little Doris Hutton, who has been missing from her home since the 31st of July, has been abandoned since the child's blue knitted cap has been found near the old mine shaft. It was feared from the first that she might have wandered in that direction, but though the searchers went over the ground more than once the cap escaped notice. The shaft is fenced in but it is thought that little Doris climbed over to reach some blackberries growing on the edge of the pit and over-balanced. The authorities are of opinion that attempts to recover the body would be attended with danger and that they would be useless. Much sympathy is felt locally for the bereaved parents. Mrs. Hutton, however, has not given up hope. She refuses to believe that Doris fell down the shaft, though she agreed that the cap was one she had herself knitted for the child. . . . 'Doris was only four,' she says, 'and the pit is over two miles from our cottage. She would never have strayed so far, a little thing like that.' Little Doris was very popular with her school mates, and the tragedy has thrown a gloom over the village."

"Very sad," said Sir James, "but what's the connection?"

"I'm coming to that, sir. Sergeant Garroway, following Collier's instructions, rang up local house agents. There was a furnished house to let on the outskirts of Mardlescombe. It was taken last year for three months by Mrs. Maulfry."

Nobody spoke for a moment. Then Sir James drew a long breath.

"Look here, are you hinting that Mrs. Maulfry kidnapped this child?"

"I'm not hinting at all, sir," said his subordinate in his most wooden manner, "but Collier told Garroway to look out for a certain class of case on a certain date, and then find out if any of the people he named were in the neighbourhood at the time. There's no 'int about that." Suppressed emotion made havoc of Cardew's aspirates.

"A certain date," mused the R.A. "The thirty-first of July."

And then, "Good God! That's to-night. This is the thirty-first."

"Yes, sir," said Cardew. "That's why—begging your pardon—I can't go home to my bed. I promised Collier I'd stand by, and I'm doing that, but I'd like to do more."

He looked at the Assistant Commissioner.

Sir James had turned rather white under his tan. He was pulling nervously at his short grey moustache.

"Damn it all, Cardew, I agree it sounds pretty sinister, but it's all supposition. Confound you, man, don't stand there like an image." He checked himself. "I'm sorry, but the whole business is so motiveless. Collier may know what he's after, but I don't. And you're asking me to involve my department. Make no mistake about this, Cardew. If we interfere with these people and fail to justify that interference they will almost certainly break us."

"Yes, sir. I told Collier that the other day. I warned him. I thought myself then that he'd found a mare's nest. Now—it's for you to say, sir."

"And if I say file any evidence you've got for future reference and leave it at.that? In other words—drop it?"

Sir James looked hard at his subordinate. The Superintendent turned very red. "I—I'm sorry, sir, but this has come to mean a good deal to me since I saw these newspaper cuttings. I'd have to leave—"

Sir James raised his eyebrows. "Resign? Nonsense, Cardew. You've been overworking. You'll take a different view of this in the morning. I've been patient because I know that both you and Collier mean well, but there is no connection between these accidents. That must be obvious to any unprejudiced observer. If we carry on this enquiry we shall be guilty of wasting the taxpayer's money. No—" He held up his hand, seeing that Cardew was about to speak. "Don't say anything now that you will regret to-morrow. Is there anyone beside Collier at work on this fantastic case?"

"Garroway and four assistants were looking up the newspaper files, but they've all gone off duty. There's nobody else—but I promised to stand by and let him have all the men he needed."

"You needn't worry about that. He won't need them. The whole thing is more or less the creation of poor Collier's overheated fancy. He'd better be seen by the doctor when he reports at the Yard. He's excitable—I haven't been quite happy about him." Sir James looked at his watch. "I must be off. Now, Cardew." He had got up from his chair, and he laid a friendly hand on the burly Superintendent's shoulder; "don't take anything I have said amiss. You came to me for my opinion and you've got it. If I'm wrong the responsibility is mine. No one can blame you. You live at Kew, don't you? I'm driving out that way. I'll give you a lift home. Come along. Good night, Spenlowe; good night, Cuffe; good night, Smith. We rely on your discretion, mind. Not a word of this to anyone."

There was a chorus of good nights. Cuffe got up and went over to the window. He was in time to see Sir James get into his car which was parked outside. The Superintendent got in beside him. Sir James was driving himself.

Spenlowe joined him. *"Sic transit gloria mundi,"* he said. "It has been given to us to witness the deflation of a super. I never saw a man wilt more rapidly. It was really pitiable. He'll come down on the other fellow, the one under him, like a steam roller, to even things up."

"I suppose so," said the artist absently. "He certainly looked unhappy. But, you know, Spen, he was in earnest. I—to tell you the truth I don't feel very happy myself."

The other stared. "You don't believe that rigmarole?"

Cuffe's habitual rather boisterous high spirits seemed to have deserted him. His gravity was all the more impressive for being so unlike him. "I don't want to," he said, "but I'm afraid I do."

CHAPTER XX
ON BOARD THE "HALCYON"

A RAY of light from an electric torch travelled slowly round the saloon of the yacht, resting for a moment on the overturned table and that shattered glass on the Persian rug, until it reached the somewhat dishevelled figure of Collier, leaning against the bookcase. He had pulled a volume from the shelves and was prepared to launch it at the newcomer, but his ankles and wrists were still tingling and numb and he found it difficult to stand without support.

"What's all this?" The voice behind the torch was not friendly, but it sounded official, and Collier's spirits rose.

"Are you a policeman? Switch that thing off, for Heaven's sake. You're blinding me."

"Hold up your hands."

Collier obeyed. A switch clicked and the softly shaded lights in the ceiling went on. He saw a young constable standing in the doorway. He jumped to the conclusion that his Superintendent, after thinking over their brief talk over the telephone, had decided he might need help at this end and had got into touch with the county police.

"Jolly good of you to come along so promptly," he said. "There's been a spot of trouble here. They knocked me out and tied me up and I've only just been able to cut myself free. I was afraid when I heard you coming down the companion that they were coming back to finish the job." He was talking too much in his relief, and his volubility made an unfavourable impression on the young constable.

"You can tell the Inspector all about that at the station," he said. "The less you say now the better. And I'd advise you to come quiet and not try and give me the slip. There's been a lot of this pilfering from yachts at anchor."

Collier's face fell. So the Superintendent was leaving him to carry on alone. Well, he could not complain. He had asked for it.

"What makes you think I've no business on board?" he asked. "I might be the owner."

The policeman grinned. "Nothing doing. I know the owner by sight, and the crew. Come on now."

"Oh damn," said Collier feelingly. The constable was quite right, of course, but it was maddening to be held up like this when every minute was precious. He was feeling rotten, too. There was a pile of luggage by the bookcase, waiting, no doubt, to be taken to the different cabins. He sank down on a large dress basket.

It creaked protestingly under his weight.

"Now then," urged his captor. "I got to get back on my beat."

"All right—just a minute."

Once more Collier crouched forward, his head nearly on his knees, trying to overcome his growing faintness. His sensations were not merely physical, though his fall earlier in the evening and the rough handling he had had since contributed to what he feared might be a complete collapse. He was aware, besides, of a dark oppression of his spirit, a kind of sick recoil from some horror that was not manifest to his senses.

The young policeman eyed him uneasily. "You'll feel better when we get on deck," he said, "it's a bit stuffy down here."

He took Collier's arm and helped him to his feet. Collier made no resistance. The sooner they got to the station the better. If they had not heard from Cardew there he would have to ring up Headquarters. If only his head were clearer. As he got to his feet he had seen something that he knew was significant though his tired brain refused to let him understand why. A clue, surely. Presently, when he felt more like himself, he would return to it.

He recovered himself a little when they came on deck. As in a dream he saw the lights of the Brighton road reflected in the oily black water of the harbour. The journey from the water side to the police station seemed longer than it actually was. Once arrived there were dazzling unshaded lights and the familiar smell of carbolic soap, and, to his immense relief, a man he knew. The recognition was mutual.

"Good God! Collier, what's happened? A road accident? Lay him down, constable, on that bench. Brandy—"

When the mists cleared away Collier found himself alone with his friend in the latter's shabby little office.

"So you got your stripes, Timson. Fancy you being down here."

"I got transferred from the Metropolitan Division. London didn't suit my wife. She's delicate, unfortunately. And her people come from this part. And now what's at the back of P.C. Wade's report? We've had complaints from boat owners of things being stolen. He tells me he heard a crash from the cabin of a yacht and found you below and that you told him some yarn about being knocked out and tied up."

"Quite right. I'm on a case—"

"What sort of a case?"

"Call it kidnapping. That boat comes into it. There's something damnably wrong."

The other interrupted. "If it's the *Halcyon* we know the owner, have known him for years. He's a very rich man and a real good sort. Why he gave one of the challenge cups at the police sports last year. It must be some other craft."

"It was the *Halcyon* all right."

"There must be some mistake. He's had the same crew ever since he's been coming here. We've nothing against them."

"Oh, all right," said Collier wearily. "You haven't had a call from the Yard this evening?"

"We certainly haven't. About this affair?"

"Yes. I'll have to get through at once. Am I keeping you up?"

"You are. But it doesn't matter for once. I can get on with some arrears of work. When you were brought in I let them know at home that I might be detained some time."

Collier got through with rather less than the usual delay, but Timson, listening to the one-sided conversation that followed was hardly surprised by the burst of profanity with which Collier relieved his feelings as he hung up the receiver.

"See here, old chap," he said not unkindly, when the C.I.D. man paused for breath. "You're tired and done up. I'm sorry I haven't a spare room, but we can make you up a bed in here with a pillow and a couple of rugs, and you can sleep until seven when I'll leave word for someone to bring you a nice hot cup of tea; and then when you've had a bath and a good breakfast we'll talk things over and see what can be done."

Collier stared at him for a moment in silence. Then he laughed. "I believe you think I'm off my rocker. I'm not. Look here, Timson. My Superintendent sent for me this morning about this case. I was to carry on and he was to stand by and send help if I needed it. Now when I ring up I'm told that he's gone home and left no instructions. The super! I've had the rough edge of his tongue often enough, but he's never let me down. Never. I wouldn't have believed it of him."

"Too bad," said Timson, "but it's late you know, old fellow. I'll have that bed made up. You'll feel tons better in the morning."

He started involuntarily as Collier, who had been prowling restlessly round the room, whirled round to face him.

"Timson," he said earnestly, "I beg of you, I beg of you to come back with me now to the yacht. Bring one of your men. There's something there I must show you. I saw it and didn't realise what it meant. We were pals in the days when we were raw recruits together. I ask this as a favour. Don't say no!"

Timson hesitated. He was still almost certain that he had to deal with a man whose mind had given way. It was very distressing. He had always liked and admired Collier.

"Very well," he said, "my motor cycle and sidecar's in the yard. Wade has gone back to his beat. We can pick him up if we see him on the road."

They found Wade within a hundred yards of their destination. Within ten minutes of leaving the station they were on the *Halcyon*'s deck.

"Don't the crew ever sleep on board when she's at anchor here?" asked Collier.

"Only occasionally, I think. Mr. Quayle's easy going, I imagine. I've seen them in the distance polishing the brass work and so on. Do you know them at all, Wade?"

"I spoke to one of them once, sir. He only grinned. The barmaid at the Sailor's Rest says they're deaf and dumb."

"What? All four of them?"

"That's what she says. I don't know."

Timson grunted. "What do you want to show me, Collier?"

"Lend me your torch, I've lost mine."

He led the way down the companion. Timson lingered behind to whisper to his subordinate. "I'm afraid he's a bit touched. I'm humouring him."

"Yes, sir."

Collier switched on the lights as he crossed the threshold of the saloon.

"There you are," he said, "see the overturned table? I was lying under it when I came to. I knocked it over and broke the glasses. I cut the cord at my wrist with a bit of glass. A tedious job and dangerous. I might have severed an artery but I didn't. The only piece of luck I've had tonight—except meeting you. Now, you see that pile of suit-cases and trunks? Quayle's off on a cruise to-morrow with the morning tide. He's taking a party of friends with him and their luggage was brought on board this afternoon and dumped in here. When Wade came in I sat on that dress basket. I felt awful. He helped me to stand up. That's when I saw something. Come over here—"

He bent over the basket and pointed.

Caught on an end of the plaited wicker of the lid was a long fair hair.

CHAPTER XXI
THE VIGIL

FOR some minutes after Dennis had darted into the shrubberies he could think of nothing but the cool soft texture of Celia's cheek. He had kissed her. She had let him kiss her, but he had not been able to persuade her to come away with him. And now—was anything going to happen?

Apparently not. He heard the two cars come up the drive and turn into the stable yard, and he caught a glimpse through the thick screen of the undergrowth of Celia's pale blue linen frock as she walked round to the other side of the house to meet her employer. He had told Celia he would be near if she wanted him, and he meant to keep his word. He made himself as comfortable as circumstances permitted, but the ground was hard, and, after a while, the dry rustling of the laurels began to get on his nerves. They sounded too much like furtive footfalls and whispering. Only the leaves; but he knew that if he gave way to his fancy he might come to believe that faint ceaseless gabble had some other origin. Once he thought he heard somebody within the house playing the piano, but there was no other sound or sign of life. The hours passed slowly. He grew tired of looking at his watch. The sky was covered with clouds and a few large drops of rain fell at intervals. It was oppressively hot and once at least he heard a distant rumble of thunder. He was badly bitten by midges. He longed for a cigarette but felt that it would be imprudent to light one. What had become of Collier? He had left no definite instructions. Was he—Dennis—to remain hidden in the shrubberies until the man from the Yard came back?

"The Casabianca touch," he thought. "Oh hell! I wonder if I'm making a complete ass of myself."

He shifted his ground a little and sat down again with his back to a tree trunk. He could see the house better from here. Hours and hours, and nothing had happened. He allowed his thoughts to wander. His father and Celia—she was just the sort of girl the old man liked. He would have to arrange a meeting. After that it would be all plain sailing.

He woke up with a start. It was quite dark now and a wind was sighing in the tree tops. He turned his head uneasily, trying to see into the black depths of the neglected shrubberies that lay between the house and the gate.

It was this dread of an undefined something that dogged one's steps and seemed always on the point of showing itself that had made a lasting and very disagreeable impression on his boyish mind the first time he ever entered the grounds of the Manor. He had been spending his holidays at the vicarage and his cousin Millie had dared him first to go up the lane, and then to climb the park wall to fetch the ball she had thrown over. He did not want to lose his ball, and he was not going to be called a coward by any girl.

"I'll get the ball and I'll go into the house," he had boasted.

And he had done it, but even now he did not care to recall his sensations as he walked down the long dark passages, opening and shutting doors as he went, until he reached the central hall with its red pillars supporting the gallery. He had heard of those pillars. The villagers could very seldom be induced to talk about the Manor, but the old woman who kept the tiny sweet shop had told him once that nobody knew how many there were because they could not be counted.

He had begun to count them, standing in the patch of light under the lanthorn roof. "One, two, three—"

Then, abruptly, his nerve had failed and he had got out of the house as quickly as he could. Millie was waiting for him in the lane.

"Did you see anything?"

He would not tell her. He was white and shaking. But, of course, there had been nothing. It was all imagination. Only, he realised it now, he had never really forgiven his cousin. On another occasion she had come with him, but that was only on a hurried scamper through the neglected gardens. They had not entered the house.

He stared at it now with an odd mixture of curiosity and repulsion. For a while its roof and chimneys with their cloak of ivy had been dark against the evening sky. Now their outlines were lost and he saw only the stuccoed facade glimmering vaguely through the surrounding gloom. There was some wind and shadows moved across it. The effect was strange. It reminded him of a sack full of living creatures writhing and struggling to get out. He became aware, too, of a distant murmur that might have been the sound of the wind in the trees though it seemed to him to come from within the house. For some time it rose and fell with a plangent rhythm broken at intervals by discordant cries.

There had been lights earlier in the evening for a few minutes in three of the windows that opened on what had once been a lawn, but Celia's had remained dark.

He had compared the house to a sack stuffed with living animals: now, as the wind rose in gusts and the shadows raced across it, he saw a resemblance to a balloon straining at its mooring ropes. The illusion was so strong that at one moment he would hardly have been surprised if it had soared up and away, flying before the gale.

Time passed; the wind died down and with it the sounds that had so puzzled him ceased. The dim light of a candle glimmered in several of the ground floor windows in succession, as though one person carrying a light was passing from room to room. It shone last in Celia's, and then was extinguished. With the silence and the dropping of the wind the house itself seemed to fall back, to become, as it were, deflated, mere lifeless bricks and mortar.

Dennis, who had been watching that strange involved play of flying shadows with the fascinated attention that most men give to moving water, roused himself with an effort. He realised that he had been on the verge of falling asleep again.

He struck a match, sheltering the tiny flame with his hand, and looked at his wrist watch. It was twenty minutes to twelve. The night so far had been uneventful. Nothing had happened to justify his intrusion. There was a perfectly good explanation for the sounds he had heard. Mrs. Maulfry and her friends had spent a blameless evening listening to a concert broadcast from a portable wireless set. Now it was over, and they had gone to bed.

And Celia was all right. If she had needed help she would have called out, and he would have heard her.

Still, just to reassure himself, he thought he would try to have a word with her now that she had returned to her room.

He crossed the lawn. It was so dark that he had no fear of being seen. He stepped on to the stone flagged path that surrounded the house, came to her window, and knocked on the glass.

He waited, expecting to hear some movement within, but the silence remained unbroken.

He tapped again, gently, for he was afraid of attracting the attention of the occupant of the adjoining room.

"Celia," he whispered, "it's me. Dennis."

He wanted her to open the window and scold him for having waited there all those hours, faithful and foolish as a dog outside a closed door; for imagining that there could be anything wrong and that she was not quite capable of taking care of herself. Growing impatient he knocked again, and this time a little louder. He had to have an answer of some kind. He had to know she was there, and safe.

But the window remained shut, and the house silent.

And then, as he lingered, not knowing what to do next, the moon shone for an instant through a rift in the clouds, and even as he stepped back hastily into the deeper shadow of the laurels something emerged from the last of the ground floor windows at the far end of the terrace.

Dennis gasped. He had seen—what had he seen? Not a human being certainly, and not an animal. A thing with horns that gibbered and pranced and clawed the air.

For a minute or more the young man leant against the wall, feeling sick and faint and fighting to recover his self control.

Celia. He had to think of Celia. Nothing else mattered now. He stepped back to her window and shattered one of the upper panes of glass with his elbow. He expected a startled cry from within the room, but the silence remained unbroken. It was incredible that she should sleep on unless she had been drugged.

He fumbled for the window catch, found it, and stepped into the room, noticing as he did so a peculiar acrid smell. He struck another match, and glanced about him.

The room was scantily furnished. He saw at once that the bed had not been slept in, and yet a girl's clothing lay across a chair. He recognised the blue linen frock Celia had been wearing that afternoon, and a little blue and white spotted scarf that he had often seen about her neck trailed on the dusty boards at his feet.

The match burned out, scorching his fingers. He struck another, lighting the candle that stood on the chest of drawers. There was no cupboard in the room and no wardrobe. He gave one more quick glance round and then went into the passage. He was angry now, with a fierce anger that left no room in his mind for fear. He walked down the long passage just as he had done years before when he first entered that ill-omened house, opening the doors and looking in. All were empty, though in some of them there was clothing scattered about as if it had been removed in haste.

He came to the circular entrance hall. The air here struck cold as a vault and the acrid smell he had already noticed was very strong. Dennis lifted the candle above his head. The shadows of the red pillars sprang up, black and threatening, on the walls. The door of the music room, the door leading to the servants' quarters, all the doors except the front door, stood open. There was no gleam of light anywhere, no movement save that of the shadows, and no sound.

The house had had occupants half an hour earlier. He had seen the light moving from room to room. They had not left in their cars. He would have heard the engines starting. What had happened, and where had they all gone? Where, above all, was Celia? He was more puzzled than angry now, and fear was creeping back.

He glanced about him uneasily. The shadows of the pillars leapt to the gallery as he lifted the candle. There were chalk marks on the floor, and grey ash, and scattered leaves.

Chapter XXII
A BURNING OF BOATS

Mrs. Cardew sat up in bed and listened. A car had stopped outside. She heard voices the click of the gate, and her husband's footsteps coming up the path. Mary Cardew had been married twenty years, and for fifteen of those years, until little Jeanie was born, she had mothered her man. She could interpret every twitch of those shaggy grey brows, every inflection of his voice. His tread now as he came up the path told her something. She reached for her dressing-gown, a useful flannel garment, and was downstairs and lighting the gas ring to make his cocoa as he entered the tiny hall.

"Hallo, Mary, you still up?"

"Yes."

He was filling his pipe from the tobacco jar on the mantelpiece as she came in with his supper on a tray. The jar was inscribed: A present from Littlehampton. They generally went there now for their annual holiday and spent their time sitting on the sands watching Jeanie, small, plump and determined, digging sand castles.

"I thought from what you said when you rang up that you might be all night at the Yard."

"I thought so too," he said heavily.

She glanced anxiously at his bowed shoulders. "You got a lift home."

"Yes, Sir James Mercer brought me along in his car."

"The Assistant Commissioner. Whatever for?"

"I'd been to see him at his Club, I was going back to the Yard, but he didn't approve. He said he'd drop me as he was coming this way. Naturally I couldn't say no."

"Of course not. I suppose it was quite an honour."

Cardew grunted.

"Have your supper before you start smoking, Tom."

"All right." He sat down and began to eat, but after a minute he pushed his plate away. "It turns to sand in my mouth," he complained.

"You're upset."

"Yes. I don't want cocoa. Give me a drop of whisky with hot water. How's my little lass?"

"Fast asleep."

He lit his pipe and smoked in silence for a few minutes while his wife cleared away the hardly touched supper. She came back presently and sat down. "Now, Tom, what is it?"

"Nothing," he said.

She knew better than to press him, and after a while he added,

"I made a promise and I've got to break it."

"Oh—why?"

"Orders." He looked up at her unhappily. "The chaps under me get the rough side of my tongue often enough, but I've never let one down before."

"You always do your best, Tom," said the loyal wife. "They know that."

"Aye. But this time my best hasn't been good enough."

"Would it help you to tell me about it, Tom? Get it off your chest like?"

He shook his head. "It's a long story, and we haven't come to the end of it yet. Sir James is wrong, and I ought to have stood up to him, Mary. I did try. But he let me see what it would mean. Losing my job and my pension. It wasn't only myself. I had to think of you and Jeanie, hadn't I?"

"It's—it's something frightfully serious then?" she said rather faintly.

He did not answer at once, and when he spoke the first word he uttered seemed to drop like a stone into the silence.

"Murder. Collier got on to it more or less by chance. He's been working alone so far, and without official sanction, but this morning I promised to back him up. That's the whole trouble, Mary. I've got to go back on that."

"Because the Assistant Commissioner says so?"

"That's right."

"But why? He ought to know you're not one to rush at things."

"The people involved don't belong to the underworld. They aren't crooks. If we held them and couldn't prove our case there'd be the devil to pay. It seemed to me we ought to take the risk. Sir James thought differently. That's that."

He knocked the ashes out of his pipe and stood up. "You'd better nip back to bed, old lady. You'll be catching a chill."

"Are you coming?"

"No. But I'll just have a look at Jeanie."

"Take off your shoes then."

She carried the supper things out to the scullery for the little maid to deal with in the morning while her husband crept upstairs to stand for a minute by his little girl's cot.

Jeanie, flushed with sleep, burrowing her tousled flaxen head into the pillow, seemed, for once, to have a depressing effect on her proud father. He looked gloomier than ever when he came down again. Mrs. Cardew took fright when she saw his face.

"What's the matter? You don't think she's feverish?"

"No, no. Jeanie's all right, bless her. She's safe. But there are other children. There's a little girl in this case, Mary. If Collier's right she's in danger. Mary"—there was a note of appeal she had rarely heard in his voice—"suppose it was Jeanie and some cop, who might have saved her, stood by and did nothing because he'd had his orders and was afraid of being sacked for disobedience?"

She moistened her lips. "Do what you think right, Tom. Never mind the consequences. I won't blame you, whatever happens."

His face cleared. "Thank you, my dear. That's what I wanted." He slipped an arm about the sturdy little figure in the grey flannel dressing gown. "Give me a kiss, old girl. And now I've got to get through a trunk call. You might get me a thermos of tea and cut some sandwiches."

"Are you going back to the Yard?"

"No. Sir James said not. I'm going to try to get in touch with Collier now."

Twenty minutes later Cardew was running the smart little Austin Seven in which he took his wife and Jeanie out for trips into the country out of the garage. Mary, passing in the thermos and the sandwiches, did not fail to notice an unusual bulge in his right hand coat pocket. She made no comment, but when he had gone and she went back into the house she looked in the top right hand drawer of her husband's bureau, and found, as she had expected, that the wicked little black automatic he kept there was gone.

"Oh dear," she thought, "I hope I was right to let him go."

Cardew meanwhile, had already crossed the river. Richmond, Kingston bye-pass, and a chance to get a move on.

At Lewes they had no news for him, but then he was not sure if a visit to the local police station had been a part of Collier's programme. "And I can't go through Sussex with a fine tooth comb," thought the Superintendent ruefully. There were the Garlands. He stopped at an A.A. telephone box. He was methodical and as a matter of routine he had made a note of their number when Collier referred to them in the course of his report. He was answered by John Garland.

"I am Superintendent Cardew, speaking from an A.A. box. Can you tell me the present whereabouts of Inspector Collier?"

"He left here after lunch with my son. They were going to Belgrave Manor. I haven't seen or heard of either of them since. Frankly, I'm getting the wind up, Superintendent. Shall I get in touch with the police here?"

"I'd rather you waited a little longer. Collier rang up the Yard at eight o'clock from a road house called Susan's Parlour. He was on his way to Shoreham."

"Was my son with him?"

"He didn't say. He was in a great hurry."

"If anything happens to my son I shall hold the police responsible. Why the hell can't you do your own dirty work? What do we pay rates for?"

"All right, sir. Steady on. No need to get worried. We'll look after your young man," said Cardew soothingly. "I'll ring you up again before long." But he was in a cold sweat of apprehension as he left the box and got into his car. Only one thing was clear to him. Collier had gone down to Shoreham because Sebastian Quayle's yacht was there.

During the summer months the main roads leading from London to the south coast are never clear of traffic, but at that hour they were not congested, and Cardew, usually inclined to over caution, rushed on that night like a man possessed. Fear is infectious and he had realised that John Garland was afraid. He had taken the Brighton road and he came to the little old harbour town six miles to the westward of that paradise of trippers by the coast road through Portslade.

The road was up at a bend and a string of lanthorns glimmered like a necklace of rubies. A quarter of a mile farther on his headlights revealed the stalwart figure of a young policeman standing apparently on guard by a door in the palings of a yard leading to the water's edge. Cardew stopped with a grinding of brakes and the constable moved forward.

"I want to find a yacht, *Halycon*, owned by Mr. Sebastian Quayle."

"She's moored just here, sir, if you'll come this way."

"Oh—is there anyone on board her now?"

The policeman was holding the gate open. "This way, sir," he repeated.

Cardew grinned. "Not giving anything away, are you? Quite right, my lad."

His companion had shut the gate and wedged it with a block of wood before he led the way across the yard to the flight of rotting wooden steps that gave access to a private jetty. The yacht, moored alongside, glimmered palely through the darkness. A light shone through the portholes of her saloon. Superintendent Cardew, who disliked boats and knew nothing about them, clambered on board gingerly in the wake of his guide.

"One moment, constable, before I go down, I want to know who's there."

"Are you one of the party that's expected, sir? A friend of the owner?"

"I am not." A natural reluctance to burning his boats had prevented Cardew from announcing himself before. He was here against his superior's orders and once he gave his name there could be no turning back. All the consequences of his act of flat disobedience flashed through his mind. The loss of his job, the loss of his pension, Mary, Jeanie. . . . But the pause he made was hardly perceptible.

"I am Superintendent Cardew, of New Scotland Yard."

The young policeman sprang to attention and saluted. "Beg pardon, Superintendent, I wasn't to know."

"Of course not. I've no complaints. But tell me now what's up here."

"I heard a noise on board about an hour ago. The owners of some of the other craft have been complaining of pilfering going on. I found a man in the saloon. There was a table knocked over and a lot of broken glass, and he said he'd been attacked and tied up and left by the party that had motored him down. He gave his name and asked me to take him along to the station. I did that and came back to my beat. About a quarter of an hour ago he came along here again with our Inspector. I was told to stay by this gate and keep my eyes open."

"Did this man give the name of Collier? Inspector Collier?"

"He did."

"Good. You can go back to your post."

As Cardew descended the steep and narrow flight of stairs to the saloon the door below opened and the light of an electric torch was flashed in his face.

"Thank the Lord!" There was heart-felt relief in that voice, ragged with fatigue. "It's the superintendent himself. Timson, this is Superintendent Cardew, come down from the Yard. That'll show you—"

Cardew shook hands with the local man. "What's been going on here?"

Collier answered ruefully. "I rang you up from that road house. I was offered a lift just afterwards and never tumbled to it that the obliging youth was one of the gang. Of course he heard me at the telephone and put two and two together. When he got me down here he bashed me over the head, tied me up and left me. You see all the luggage they've brought on board. We saw the girl at the Manor this afternoon and she told us they were starting on their cruise to-morrow. Inspector Timson says the tide will be right about six."

Cardew grunted. "What about the child, the little girl? You say you saw the governess?"

"Yes. She said the kid's mother had fetched her away. She's staying on with Mrs. Maulfry to take the place of the girl who was killed in the street last night."

"Does she know the other secretary is dead?"

"No. Young Garland tried to persuade her to come away, but she wouldn't. She won't hear a word against her employer. The whole crowd came back then in two cars, so Garland took cover, and I beat it. They'd been down here to bring the luggage on board."

"Is that all?" asked Cardew heavily. "I mean—you didn't find anything that would give us a line on what they're up to?"

"Nothing in the Manor. But I hadn't time to search thoroughly."

The three men stood talking under the shaded lights in the luxurious cabin, talking in anxious undertones. Cardew made no effort to conceal his disappointment.

"Then we may as well clear out of this," he said gruffly. "We can't hold these birds on suspicion. We need evidence. They tied you up—but you had no right on board without a warrant. You've done your best, Collier, and failed. Come along. We may catch them another time."

"That crew of Mr. Quayle's may be here any time if they're sailing at daybreak," said the local Inspector, "if we're going I suggest we go now. On the other hand"—he glanced rather uncertainly at Collier—"the Inspector's got an idea."

"That's his trouble," said Cardew sourly, "but we may as well hear it."

"All right, sir. Come over here."

They followed him to the corner by the door leading to the staterooms where the luggage was stacked. "I was just showing this to Inspector Timson when we heard you coming down the stairs."

He stooped to detach the long fair hair caught on the rough corner of the old basket trunk behind the pile of suit-cases.

"Lady Sabina's a platinum blonde, but this hair is too long to be one of hers. See how fine it is. Like gossamer." His voice had grown curiously gentle as he brooded over it. Cardew glanced at him quickly. "What are you getting at, Collier?"

He had placed the long silky hair in an envelope and slipped it into his note case. "Will you just lift the end of this basket to test its weight, sir?"

Cardew tried it. "Heavyish," he pronounced. "Must be something more than clothing in here. Books, perhaps."

"I want to open it and see."

Cardew eyed the trunk thoughtfully. "Not to be opened on the voyage apparently," he said. "Strongly corded, and a lump of sealing wax on every knot. You're right, Collier, there's something about this that doesn't fit in with a pleasure cruise."

He brought out a clasp knife and cut the cords with feverish haste, Collier helping him, while the local man stood by looking on with a growing uneasiness.

Cardew lifted the lid.

"Gosh," he muttered, "what does this mean?"

He heard Collier beside him draw a long breath.

The trunk was filled with a little girl's clothing, not folded but stuffed in at random with shoes and toys. Thor and Dennis Garland would have recognised Allie's red beret, and the golliwog doll that was her inseparable companion sprawling forlornly face downwards among the little crumpled frocks.

"But there's nothing heavy in all this stuff," said Cardew.

Cautiously he pried in the mass. They saw his face change.

"Good Lord! It's weighted with stones!"

He held out a large flint on the palm of his hand for their inspection.

"Plenty of those along the beach or up on the Downs," said Timson, "but what on earth—I mean—"

"They don't carry any junk on board a yacht like this," said Collier. It was the first time he had spoken since the opening of the trunk. "I think Mrs. Maulfry and her dear friend Mr. Quayle were looking ahead when they packed this little lot. This clothing is creased, but it isn't stained or torn. If Luna came and fetched her child away why didn't she take her clothes and her toys?"

Cardew looked at him. "Is this what you expected to find."

"No, it isn't, but it shows I'm on the right track. How many men have you brought along with you, sir?"

"None," said Cardew curtly. He saw Collier's face fall and added, "I daresay we can borrow a constable or two from Inspector Timson here."

"Certainly," said Timson, "but—the contents of this trunk are unusual, but it isn't a criminal offence to pack stones."

"I can't explain now," said Collier, "you'll have to trust us. The superintendent wouldn't be here if it wasn't serious, would he?"

"What do you want done, Collier?" asked the Superintendent.

"I want the constable at the gate taken away and men posted inside the yard to arrest everyone who comes on board. I want as many more men as you can spare—you'll need four for the job here—and a couple of cars. We've got to go back to the Manor, and what's more, there isn't a minute to lose."

CHAPTER XXIII
THE HORNED GOD

As DENNIS came down the stairs his candle, which had burned down to a wick flaring in a pool of wax, gave one final splutter and went out, leaving him in darkness. It had lasted long enough to enable him to make a thorough examination of every room on the upper floor. He had found no one up there, and no traces of recent occupation. He felt for the banisters and made his way down to the hall. He had to accept the fact that for some extraordinary reason the house had been abandoned by its occupants at some time after one o'clock in the morning. They had not left in their cars for he would have heard them if they had. Had they gone back over the Downs to Susan's Parlour to finish the night there? But would they take Celia with them in that case? She had undressed—

Dennis set his teeth. He had to find her, and quickly. He bumped into a pillar in the dark and swore. The strange acrid smell, stronger in the hall than elsewhere, made him feel oddly light-headed. He struck a match and sheltering the flame with his hand, peered through the open doorway of the music room. He saw Mrs. Maulfry's piano, the divan round the walls, the scattered cushions. The match flickered out. He turned back to the hall and lit another. Those chalk marks on the dusty boards were not drawn at random. A circle and two interlinked triangles. There were some letters too, partly effaced. Suddenly, he could not have said why, he thought of the derelict chapel on the hill side and the fragments of the broken stone cross fallen in a bed of nettles.

"Tommy rot!" he said aloud, and was so startled by the sound of his own voice breaking that uncanny silence that he nearly dropped the match box. Well, he had done with the house anyway. He tried the front door, found it unlocked and unbolted, and stepped out under the portico. He went round by way of the stable yard to make sure that he was not mistaken about the cars. They were both there, Quayle's Bentley and Mrs. Maulfry's Rolls. He was about to strike his last match to examine the interior of the Rolls when the silence of the night was broken by a long drawn plaintive cry.

The scream of a rabbit caught in a snare? But no poacher in that countryside would dream of setting his wires on Belgrave Down.

"Oh, God!" muttered Dennis. The cry came from the hill side. He ran across the yard and stumbled up the steps to the kitchen garden, plunging wildly in the darkness through a jungle of currant and gooseberry bushes. The door in the wall was swinging on its hinges. He passed out on to the open hill side.

The cry had not been repeated but a sound of distant voices singing in a minor key was borne to him on the wind. It seemed to come from higher up, from the solitary wastes where the gale plucked and tore at the stunted juniper bushes that spring from the graves of prehistoric men.

Dennis hurried on, keeping to the faintly marked sheep track he had followed more than once with little Allie and her governess. It was a stiff climb from the Manor and his heart was thumping against his ribs. The wind screamed in his ears and seemed to be thrusting him back. He was making for the derelict church and he saw it presently, the long roof like the body and the squat tower like the lifted head of some primeval monster, dark against the first faint glimmer of light in the east. At the same moment he was aware of something that moved in a circle with a strange and sluggish rhythm, coiling like a huge snake among the forgotten graves. His labouring heart seemed to miss a beat and a cold sweat broke out on his forehead. A circle, and its centre the stone box enclosed by rusty railings, and half buried in nettles, called the Squire's Tomb.

The railings at one end had been broken down and something loomed there, black and threatening, half human and half animal, with great branching horns swaying to the infernal rhythm of the plangent chorus. Dennis, approaching at right angles to the sunken path that led up from the lane, could just discern that something like a heap of discarded clothing lay on the flat stone slab that closed the tomb.

The circle was contracting as the horned beast rose to its full height and stooped as if to strike. Simultaneously there was a sharp crack that might have been the breaking of a twig underfoot. The towering figure lost its fierce momentum, toppled sideways, and fell headlong.

There was an instant of stricken silence. Then the night was horribly rent with shrieks and howls as the circle broke and scattered.

Dennis, though he was badly shaken, put on a spurt. He scrambled over the broken wall. Twice he fell, stumbling over the mounds hidden in the long grass, but he was up again in a moment. The outcry had ceased as suddenly as it had broken out. Four men were clambering up the bank from the sunk track and crashing through the hedge of hornbeams. They reached the tomb almost as soon as he did, and the foremost switched a ray of light from an electric torch on the slab. They all saw Celia lying there, white-faced and still.

Cardew bent over her. "She's not dead. Unconscious. Drugged, I think. But look at that!" With a shaking finger he pointed to the circle daubed in red paint over her heart.

"Good God!" muttered Timson. He licked his lips. "Was—is this what you expected? What does it mean?"

"Thank Heaven we were in time," said Collier.

Dennis Garland said nothing. He could not have spoken just then if his life had depended on it. He was too profoundly moved. He pulled off his coat and wrapped it about Celia's inert body before he raised her in his arms.

The big Superintendent nodded approvingly. "That's right. You look after her. But don't try to move her yet. We'll carry her down to the car presently, but there's work to be done first."

"Beg pardon, sir," the young constable Timson had brought with him spoke for the first time and his voice was not quite under control. "That—that thing we saw reared up on the tomb is lying here among the nettles. I—I think it's moving."

The grey light of dawn was spreading in the east. They could see one another now, though dimly. Collier, after one quick glance at the speaker's face, laid a reassuring hand on his arm.

"Steady," he said quietly. "This is a damnable business, but there's nothing about it that can't be explained. That was a man. Come and see for yourself."

He moved round to where, at the head of the tomb, the nettles grew, rank and luxuriant, almost to the height of the railings. Cardew followed, after a barely perceptible hesitation, and Timson and his subordinate brought up the rear. The acrid odour of crushed and trodden nettles mingled with that other sicklier smell that Dennis had noticed earlier that night when he searched the Manor. They stared at the black, shaggy, shapeless figure that sprawled, face downwards, in the narrow space between the tomb and the enclosing rails. It lay there, broken, like some grotesque toy unbearably magnified.

Timson shuddered. "What is it?" he muttered.

Collier answered. "The Grand Master of the coven. A man dressed in a black goat's skin. Don't be afraid of it," he added harshly, "it won't do any more mumming this side of hell."

He stooped and turned the body over with less of gentleness than he had ever used towards the dead.

The face that grinned up at them was so horrible that the young constable shrank back, covering his eyes, and even the Superintendent paled.

"It's a mask," said Collier quickly, "he was representing the horned god. I saw a picture of one like it yesterday. The Dorset Ooser. Look here!" He lifted the clenched right hand and showed them the two-edged blade of an obsidian knife. "That's the ritual weapon. If you hadn't shot him, Superintendent—"

Cardew cleared his throat. "I only meant to wing him," he said uneasily. "Are you sure he's done for, Collier?"

"It's the best thing that could have happened," said Collier implacably, "he wasn't fit to live."

"That may be," said the older man heavily, "but there'll be trouble over this. Who is it?"

"One of that woman—Mrs. Maulfry's crowd. They're all rotten to the core. Streete, or that Belgian professor, or Quayle himself."

"What about the others," interrupted Timson. "There were a whole lot of them up here. Oughtn't we to try to round them up?"

"Hark!" Collier, who had been fumbling over the leather straps that attached the mask, held up his hand. "Can't you hear them? They've piled into their cars."

They all listened and they all heard the sound of a car's exhaust dying away far down the valley.

"Fine," said Collier grimly. "They'll drive straight into the trap. Your men, Timson, will mop them up as they go on board the yacht."

"You're right," said Cardew, "get that mask off. Let's see who the fellow is."

"All right, Superintendent. It almost certainly isn't Quayle. I remember Quayle's hands. Plump and white. It may be no one we should recognise." He unfastened the last of the straps and lifted the mask from the still face.

Nobody spoke. The two detectives from the Yard stood as if paralysed. Timson looked from one to the other in growing alarm. He realised that they had suffered a shock for which they were unprepared. He glanced again curiously at the dead man, a man apparently between forty and fifty, with regular features and a small grey moustache.

"I see you know him," he said, "who is it?" The big Superintendent made a visible effort. He swallowed twice before he spoke. "Never mind that now, Timson. The less said the better. You understand. I'll get you two to help young Garland carry that poor girl down the hill to our car. You'd better speak to the boy, Collier. He knows you. He seems dazed, and no wonder."

Collier obeyed. Dennis, who had seemed unaware of what had been passing, lifted haggard eyes from a rapt contemplation of the girl's unconscious face.

"She—she's not coming round. Her hands are like ice."

"She will," said Collier, with more confidence than he felt. "We'll get her away now. The question is where to?"

The young man made the expected reply. "To my house, of course. Where else? We're going to be married as soon as possible."

"Right. These are friends. They'll help you carry her down to the car. Will you stay in Lewes, Timson, and get in touch with your people at Shoreham? The constable can bring the car back for us. What's your name?"

"Ayling, sir."

"You should be back in about an hour from now, Ayling. Come up the lane as far as the entrance gate to the Manor and sound your horn three times."

"Very good, sir."

"And don't talk about this to anyone. I'll be seeing you both later. You understand, Timson?"

"I'm hanged if I do," said the Inspector frankly, "but I'll keep my mouth shut."

"Good-bye."

The Superintendent stood watching the three men as they moved away, carrying Celia between them, until they vanished from sight behind the bank with its fringe of elder bushes and hornbeam. Then he turned to his colleague. Collier, looking at him, thought that in the last twelve hours he had aged as many years, but he was in no better case himself. Both men were physically spent, but that was not all.

"I was right, wasn't I, not to tell Timson? This will have to be hushed up, Collier. It will have to be. I—I suppose I can't have been deceived by a chance resemblance?"

It was broad daylight now, but the sun had risen unseen behind a bank of clouds. The wind had dropped and a fine cold rain was falling. Cardew buttoned up his coat and turned up the collar as he moved round the tomb to the end where the body of the man he had shot lay, face upwards now, with eyes that stared blindly up at the grey sky.

"No," he muttered, "I can't be mistaken. Who is it, Collier?"

Collier moistened his lips. He had some difficulty with his utterance.

"It's the Assistant Commissioner," he said. "Sir James Mercer."

CHAPTER XXIV
THE BENEFIT OF THE DOUBT

THE memorial service at St. Aldwythia's was over. The organist had played Chopin's Funeral March. Now the doors were opened and the press photographers were busy with their cameras. The Duke of Leam, hurrying down the steps to his car, tried to shield his face with his hat. A man in the crowd that had collected to watch the congregation of mourners dispersing nudged his neighbour. "Look. That's Miles Amblett, the Home Secretary."

Mr. Amblett handed his wife into their car and spoke to the chauffeur. "Home. No, Mary. I'm not coming."

One of the policemen on duty made a way for him through the crowd and beckoned to a taxi driver on the rank across the square.

Mr. Amblett got in and gave an address in Croydon.

During the drive he smoked a cigar and studied some papers he had brought with him. His face, lean, long lipped, shrewd, with the formidable jutting brows, was set in the harsh lines of physical fatigue. He had landed at Croydon only a few hours previously, having returned by air from Switzerland.

Reaching his destination he told the taxi driver to wait.

He was expected and the door was opened, before he could ring the bell by a middle-aged woman in nurse's uniform.

"They're all here, sir, in Mr. Thor's room. This way."

He followed her up the stairs to a large bedroom on the first floor. The four men who had been summoned to meet him rose as he entered. He nodded to them curtly and looked towards the bed where Cosmo Thor sat, propped up by pillows.

"I hope you are equal to this, Mr. Thor. I wanted a first hand account."

"I am convalescent. May I introduce these gentlemen to you? Mr. Dennis Garland, Superintendent Cardew, Detective-Inspector Hugh Collier. Won't you sit down, Mr. Amblett?"

"Thanks." The Home Secretary chose a chair and signed to the others to be seated. They obeyed in silence. Cardew looked more wooden than usual. The two younger men were obviously unhappy.

Mr. Amblett's cold grey eyes rested on each in turn before he began.

"I was away on my holiday when I was informed of the two recent tragedies involving in one case a relative by marriage, Miss Heriot, my wife's aunt, and, in the other the Assistant Commissioner of Police at Scotland Yard. I learnt what everybody else learnt at the same time from their newspapers. Mr. Quayle and a party of friends who were accompanying him on a cruise were on their way to Shoreham where his yacht was in harbour, early in the morning on the first of this month. Apparently the first car skidded and the second ran into it. Both seem to have been travelling at a high speed. They caught fire and all the occupants were killed. About the same time Sir James Mercer was found in his car drawn up by the road side about thirty miles away from the scene of the first disaster. He was shot through the head. The pistol was lying on the floor of the car at his feet. Apparently these tragedies were unconnected. They both took place in Sussex. That was all. In each case the inquests have been held and a verdict has been arrived at. Death by misadventure, and suicide while temporarily insane. At the enquiry into the death of Sir James it was suggested that he was suffering from overwork and too much responsibility owing to the prolonged absence of the Commissioner."

He paused while he turned over the papers on his knee. Dennis moved uneasily, but the two policemen sat like statues.

Mr. Amblett resumed, "Mrs. Amblett and I came back this morning in time to attend the memorial service held for the victims of the motor accident. Miss Heriot, as I said just now, was my wife's aunt. Lady Sabina Romaine was a cousin of the Duke of Leam. Mrs. Maulfry was widely known and respected for her charitable work. Mr. Quayle was known to lovers of art as the man who saved more than one great masterpiece for the nation."

"Quite," said a voice from the bed, "but this is not the House of Commons, Mr. Amblett."

Mr. Amblett's sallow cheeks showed a trace of colour, but he took the interruption good humouredly. "True. You do well to remind me. I'm afraid one is rather apt—" He sounded decidedly more human as he hesitated, at a loss for a word. "But all I have said about these people is true, Mr. Thor."

"Yes," said Thor quietly, "but it is not all the truth. That is suspected by some, rumoured, whispered about here and there, but known only by the four of us here present."

"I am coming to that," said Mr. Amblett. "This statement, made by Superintendent Cardew and witnessed by you all, reached me in Switzerland. It was of so startling a character, and so—I fear I must say incredible—that I thought it best to ask you to meet me here, as Mr. Thor, a material witness, is not yet able to leave his bed. This is a serious, a terribly serious matter, gentlemen. I want the truth. Any further action I may take depends on what I hear from you in corroboration of this"— he tapped the sheaf of papers on his knee—"this extraordinary narrative."

"We are here to tell you anything you want to know," said Thor.

"Yes," said the other slowly, "but it's my duty to warn you. I mean you, Superintendent. In this statement you have admitted to committing a murder."

Collier and Dennis Garland both cried out together, "No!"

Cardew said nothing. He sat with his huge hands resting on his knees, less colour than usual in his weather-beaten face, his steady blue eyes fixed on the Home Secretary.

"Well," said Mr. Amblett, "that's the point. By your admission Sir James did not shoot himself sitting in his car. He was shot by you on the hill-side some distance from the spot where he was found. You and the Inspector here carried him down to the car, staged the whole thing."

He glanced at Collier and Collier said, "Yes, sir. We didn't want him disgraced."

"Whom? Your Superintendent?"

"No, sir. Sir James."

There was a pause before Mr. Amblett answered. "Out of loyalty? I see. To avoid a scandal which I, for one, shudder to contemplate!"

"Yes, sir."

"I have held the office, the high office of Home Secretary in His Majesty's Government, since the last election. I don't take myself too seriously I hope—but my office is another matter. I have to uphold that to the best of my ability. I am trying to uphold it here, in the spirit though not in the letter. This enquiry, gentlemen, is entirely unofficial and, I have no doubt, illegal, if you regard the letter. I can't put the law in motion without bringing all these things—these horrors—to light. But some action I must take after reading Superintendent Cardew's statement—I was going to say confession, but statement is perhaps a better word. Why did you make it and send it to me, Superintendent? Were you compelled to it by those who shared your secret?"

Cardew stood up. "No, sir. It was my own idea. I couldn't be easy without telling. I didn't know who it was, and I never meant to kill him, but I had no choice. If I had to go through that night again—which God forbid—I'd do it again."

He sat down again heavily. Thor broke the ensuing silence.

"May I take it that if, on consideration, you regard the charges we have brought against Mrs. Maulfry and her friends as proved you will admit that Cardew was justified?"

Mr. Amblett turned towards the bed. "It was you who set the others on the track? You are, I understand, an authority on what are called the occult sciences?"

Thor smiled slightly for the first time. "Hardly that," he said gently. "It is a vast subject. Most people know nothing whatever about it. I know a little."

"You believe in magic, black magic?"

"I believe in forces that may be used—or misused. But that is beside the point here, Mr. Amblett. We have no evidence in this case of anything supernormal. You may call spirits from the vasty deep—but will they come? I'll give you the facts. Mrs Maulfry spent her childhood and early girlhood in Haiti. I don't know what the conditions are now, but certainly forty years ago the ancient cults were practised there. Obeah. Devil worship. It may be that she was initiated by the native servants on her father's plantation. She still owns property on the island, and so did Quayle. I think we may regard them as the leaders, the founders of a cult of satanism here. They attracted to them people like Lady Sabina Romaine, who were sated and spoiled, who had done everything and tired of everything and craved a new sensation, the sadists, the degenerate. Their influence over these followers was maintained by the use of drugs, and especially the flying ointment of which you will find mention in most old books on witchcraft, including the Grand Grimoire. Some ingredients are known, but the secret of the whole probably died with Quayle. I hope so, at any rate. I think we may assume that they formed a coven, that is, a society of eleven initiates, which, on special occasions, included a twelfth, the Grand Master, representing the horned god himself. This was the Black Man you read about in the trials of the Salem witches."

"Good Heavens!" said Mr. Amblett, "but if there were twelve of them some are still at large."

"Undoubtedly. But I think you may rest assured that the ringleaders were in those two cars, and that the survivors are very frightened people."

"Let us get this quite clear," said Mr. Amblett. "You suggest that Mrs. Maulfry got hold of this little girl, the child of this palmist, Madame Luna—what was her real name, by the way?"

"I've found that out, sir," said Collier. "It was Lunn. The birth of the child was registered at Portsmouth five years ago under that name. Alice Lunn."

"Thank you. You suggest, Mr. Thor, that these people meant to sacrifice this child to their deity?"

"I am afraid that actually happened a year ago in Somerset, Mr. Amblett. A little girl disappeared and was never found. It was believed that she had strayed on the moor and fallen down an old mine shaft—but Mrs. Maulfry and her friends were staying within three miles of the place. And the dates are significant. The 31st of July, the night of one of the four grand Sabbaths of the year."

"Good God!" Mr. Amblett produced a handkerchief and wiped his forehead. "And the child in this case?"

"Miss Kent was told that her mother had fetched her away. That was a lie, of course. At that time they hoped to allay any suspicions she might have and send her off. Little Allie had been doped with some concoction of Quayle's and was being kept in one of the rooms upstairs. She had gone to sleep quite happily, hugging her golliwog. Streete had warned Quayle to be careful with her. He had not examined her but he felt certain she was a heart subject. Quayle wouldn't listen to him. He was very proud of his knowledge of drugs, which seems indeed, to have been extensive and peculiar. When they came down to the Manor the next day she was lying where they had left her with her golliwog in her arms, very peaceful and still. When they touched her they found that she was cold. She had been dead some hours. Quayle was in a fearful state of funk. He was terrified of Mrs. Maulfry. She, meanwhile, had decided that it wouldn't be safe to let Miss

Kent go, that she knew too much—and they decided to use her instead."

"How did you learn this?"

"The Superintendent got it from Streete. He was the only one of the party who was not killed outright. He was conscious in the ambulance on the way to the hospital and the Superintendent arrived on the scene of the accident in time to accompany him and get his statement."

"I see. Did he say how they had disposed of the child's body?"

Cardew cleared his throat. "He said we'd never find it. They made two journeys to and fro to Shoreham during that day, and it may be in any pond or ditch within a thirty mile radius. We could find it right enough if we organised a search, but that would mean publicity."

"Yes. Yes. Quite," said Mr. Amblett. "Poor little child. She died in her sleep. That's one thing to be thankful for."

"Aye," said Cardew, "but Collier and I, we wanted to save her. And I ask myself how long this devilry has been going on. Every night since I've dreamed of it and waked in a cold sweat."

"And—and the other girl—Miss Kent?" said Mr. Amblett, "She has recovered from her ordeal I hope? I suppose I ought to question her."

"I hope you won't," said Thor. "She was drugged, and from what Garland tells us she has little or no recollection of what took place. It would be kind to let her forget even that little. She was fond of the child and would be heart-broken if she learned the truth. She is being well cared for and is to be married to Mr. Garland very soon."

"Really? Dear me!" said Mr. Amblett. "I hope they will be happy. I must say I welcome any gleam of light in this dark business. Terrible. Terrible. What was the motive, Mr. Thor—I still don't understand—why did they commit these crimes, run these fearful risks? Can they have taken this mumbo jumbo seriously?"

"I think so," said Thor. "The fact that these practices were dangerous, not only to others but to themselves, gave them an added interest. Spice for jaded palates. Quayle had an unappeasable curiosity, unflagging zest. They were all avid for new sensations. I wouldn't enquire into what they hoped to experience if I were you, sir. Some things are better left alone."

"I daresay you are right," said Mr. Amblett. "But—now we come to what is to me the crux of the matter. Do you seriously allege that Sir James Mercer, a man with a distinguished career behind him in India, who has for over a year held the post of Assistant Commissioner, was actually one of—of these people?"

He was speaking now to the Superintendent, and Cardew answered him.

"We had no idea of it—though he ordered us to drop the enquiry—but there he was, wearing the goatskin and the horned mask—and we found the knife in his hand. What else are we to think, sir?"

The day had been chilly for the time of year and a small fire had been lit in the grate. Mr. Amblett got up and stood on the hearthrug, looking down into the red heart of the coals.

"I can suggest a possible explanation," he said.

"It is admitted that Sir James knew these people, just as the quite large congregation present at the memorial service this afternoon knew them—as I myself did—and that he was on friendly terms with some of them. Suppose that when he heard your story, Cardew, he resolved to try what could be done by personal influence. He was, of course, horrified at the thought of the scandal, if the whole ghastly business was brought into the Courts. He drove down alone that night, thinking that he could either persuade or threaten them into dropping the whole thing. He found them maddened by the drugs in which they indulged, and the time for reasoning past. He began to hope that you had disobeyed him and that help would come. Meanwhile the only way to save the girl's life was for him to take the place of the Grand Master of the coven and try to delay the climax of their ghastly rites. When you saw him dawn was breaking and he was still playing for time—"

Cardew moistened his lips. "If that's true the word you used for me just now is right," he said huskily. "I am a murderer."

"No," said Mr. Amblett. The level voice was kinder than it had been yet. "Don't worry, Superintendent. After what I have heard I agree that you had no choice. He seemed, at least, to be about to strike, and you were not near enough to stop him in any other way. This enquiry is ended."

He folded the sheaf of papers still in his hands and, stooping, thrust them between the bars of the grate. They all watched the flame take hold of them.

"As to Sir James," said Mr. Amblett, without turning his head, "we were friends when we were young men though I have not seen much of him of late. I should be glad if you would all give him, in your minds, the benefit of the doubt."

Cardew swallowed hard. He had not dared to anticipate what the result of this conference might be.

"About me, sir—do you want me to leave the Force?"

"Leave? No, of course not. We must regard this as over and done with. Silence. I can rely on you all for that? Thank you. I thank you all." He shook hands with Thor and with the others, and left them.

They heard his step on the stairs and the closing of the front door.

Cardew passed his hand across his forehead. He hoped the others would not notice that he was trembling. "I'll be getting home," he muttered. He thought of his wife, swathed in a flannel apron, bathing Jeanie before the kitchen fire.

Dennis Garland had a train to catch. Collier was the last to leave.

"It hasn't been too tiring for you, sir," he said anxiously.

"No, not a bit. It had to be threshed out."

Collier lingered. "About Sir James—if he wasn't their Grand Master, whose place had he taken?"

The older man looked at the eager face and moved his bandaged head on the pillow. "You heard what Ablett said. Leave it." He added, half to himself, "and of your charity pray for the soul of James Mercer."

The younger man answered him humbly, "You're right, sir, of course. Good night."

Thor was alone. He lay back and closed his eyes wearily. After a minute the door was opened and his nurse peeped in.

"You've had a nice long chat with your friends," she said brightly, "and now what about a nice cup of tea?"

THE END